TEEN TITANS GO!™

IDOL HANDS AND COLD BLOODED

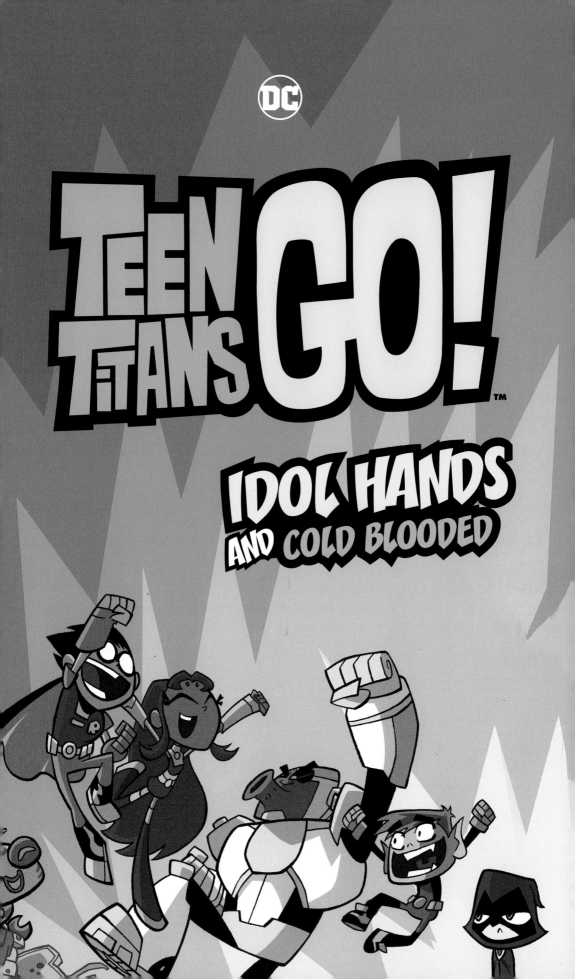

Teen Titans Go! is published by
Stone Arch Books,
A Capstone Imprint
1710 Roe Crest Drive
North Mankato, MN 56003
www.mycapstonepub.com

Library of Congress Cataloging-in-Publication Data is available at the Library of Congress website:
ISBN: 978-1-4965-7994-2 (library binding)
ISBN: 978-1-4965-8000-9 (eBook PDF)

Summary: When Starfire signs the team up for the popular reality show, *Jump City's Got Your Talent Right Here!* Robin
becomes obsessed with showing the world just how talented the Teen Titans really are! Then after a fight with Captain Cold,
Robin comes down with a cold himself! Running a high fever and quarantined from the rest of the Titans . . . the madness
begins to set in!

Alex Antone Editor – Original Series Paul Santos Editor

STONE ARCH BOOKS
Chris Harbo Editor
Brann Garvey Designer
Hilary Wacholz Art Director
Kathy McColley Production Specialist

Printed and bound in the USA
PA49

TEEN TITANS GO!™

SHOLLY FISCH MERRILL HAGAN
WRITERS

LEA HERNANDEZ JORGE CORONA
ARTISTS

JEREMY LAWSON
COLORIST

WES ABBOTT
LETTERER

DAN HIPP
COVER ARTIST

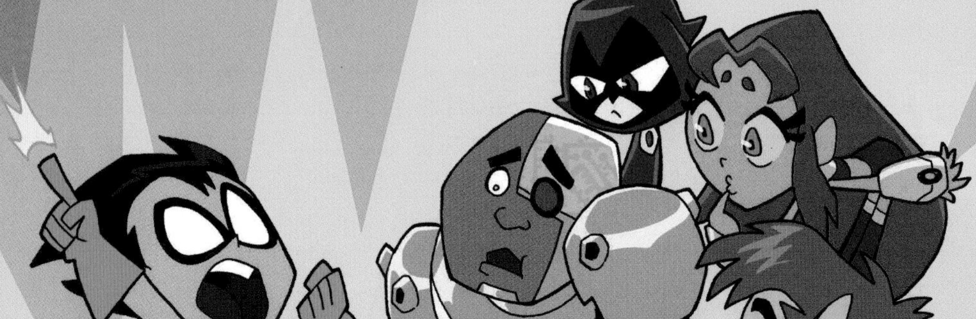

STONE ARCH BOOKS
a capstone imprint

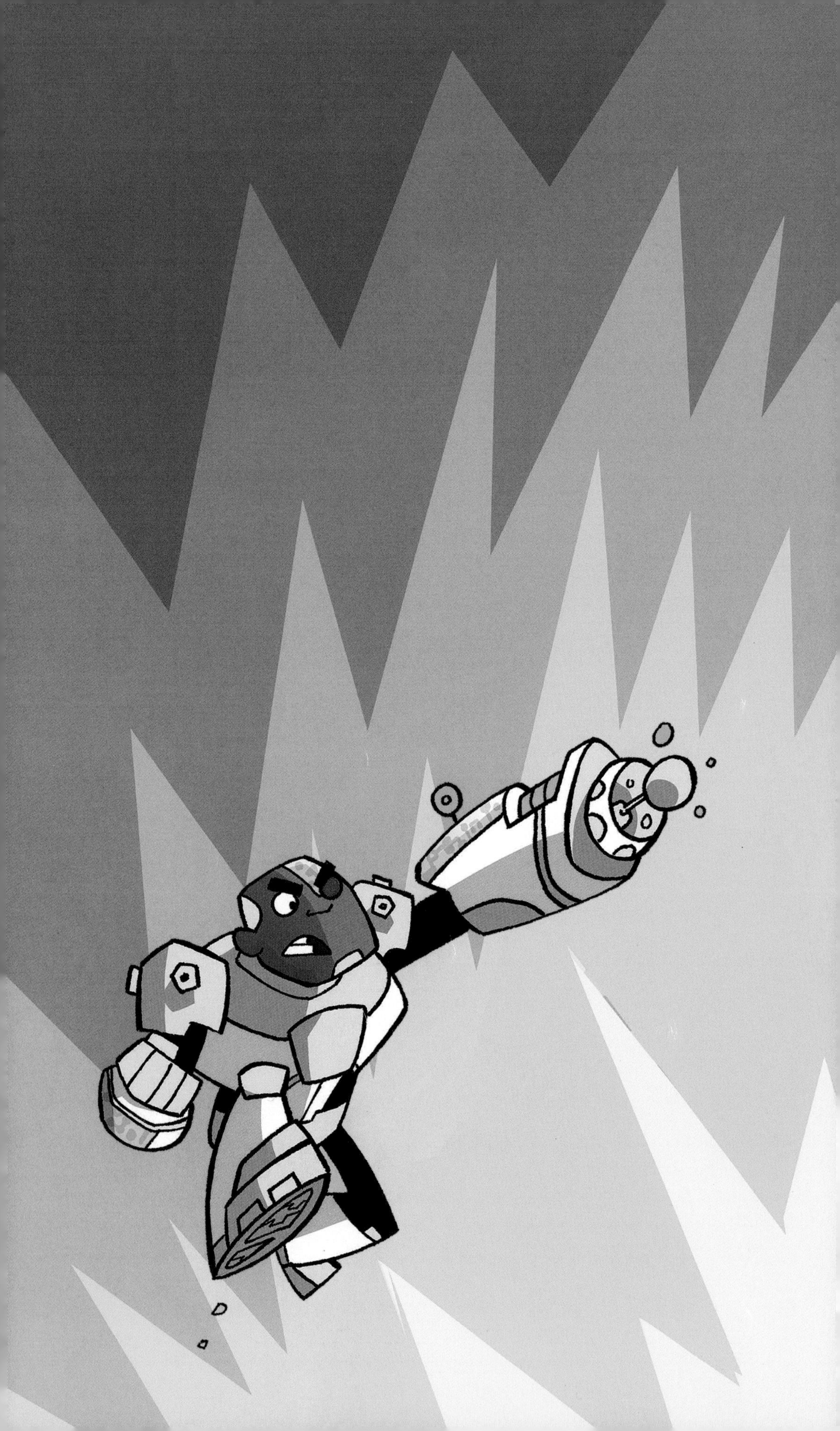

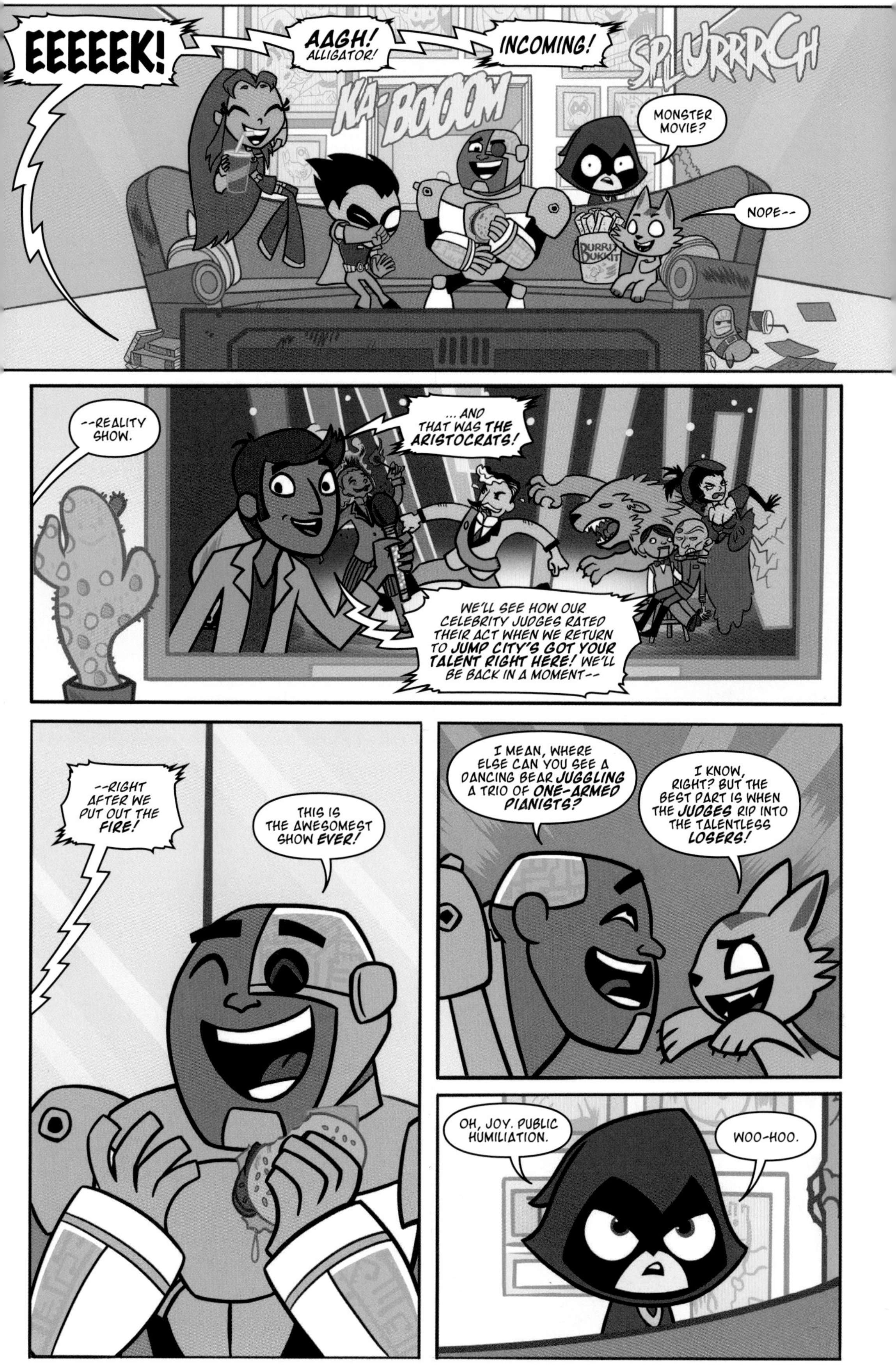
EEEEEK!
AAGH! ALLIGATOR!
INCOMING!
KA-BOOOM
SPLURRRCH
MONSTER MOVIE?
NOPE--
--REALITY SHOW.
... AND THAT WAS THE ARISTOCRATS!
WE'LL SEE HOW OUR CELEBRITY JUDGES RATED THEIR ACT WHEN WE RETURN TO JUMP CITY'S GOT YOUR TALENT RIGHT HERE! WE'LL BE BACK IN A MOMENT--
--RIGHT AFTER WE PUT OUT THE FIRE!
THIS IS THE AWESOMEST SHOW EVER!
I MEAN, WHERE ELSE CAN YOU SEE A DANCING BEAR JUGGLING A TRIO OF ONE-ARMED PIANISTS?
I KNOW, RIGHT? BUT THE BEST PART IS WHEN THE JUDGES RIP INTO THE TALENTLESS LOSERS!
OH, JOY. PUBLIC HUMILIATION.
WOO-HOO.

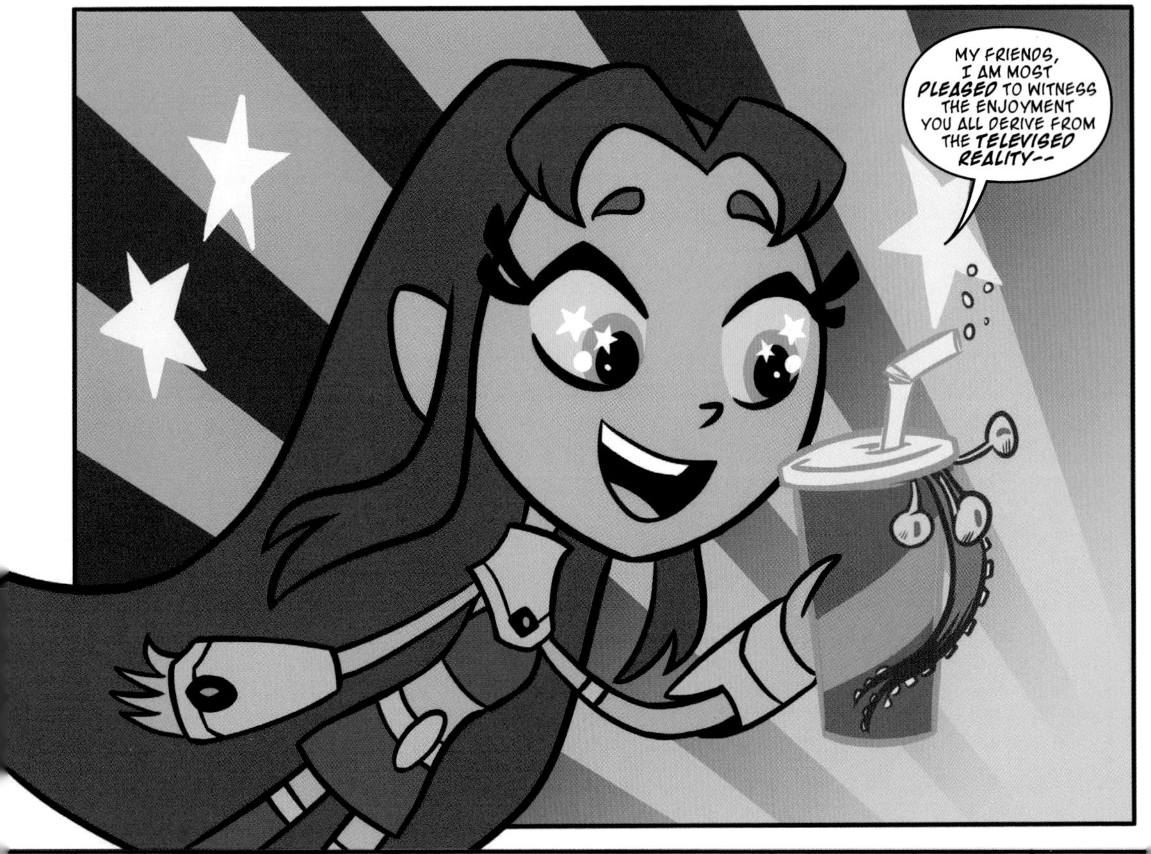
MY FRIENDS, I AM MOST PLEASED TO WITNESS THE ENJOYMENT YOU ALL DERIVE FROM THE TELEVISED REALITY--

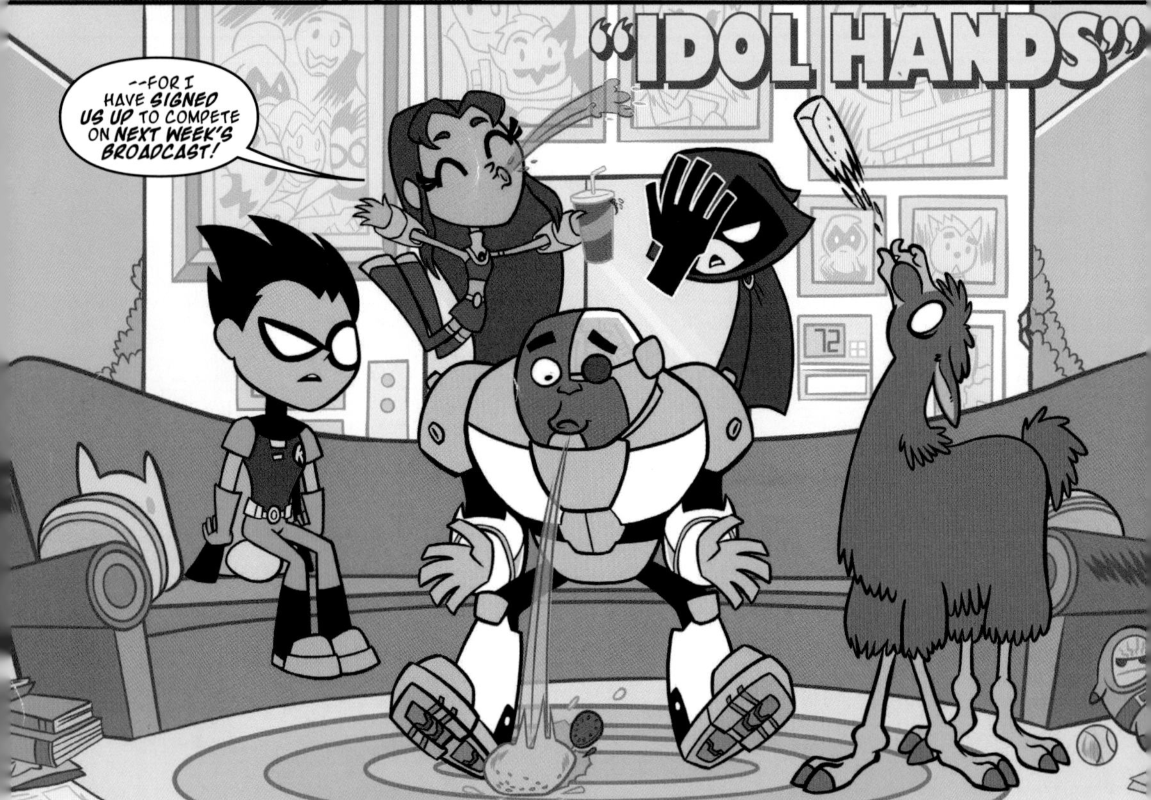
"IDOL HANDS"
--FOR I HAVE SIGNED US UP TO COMPETE ON NEXT WEEK'S BROADCAST!
72

WRITTEN BY SHOLLY FISCH ART BY LEA HERNANDEZ LETTERS BY WES ABBOTT COVER BY DAN HIPP EDITED BY ALEX ANTONE

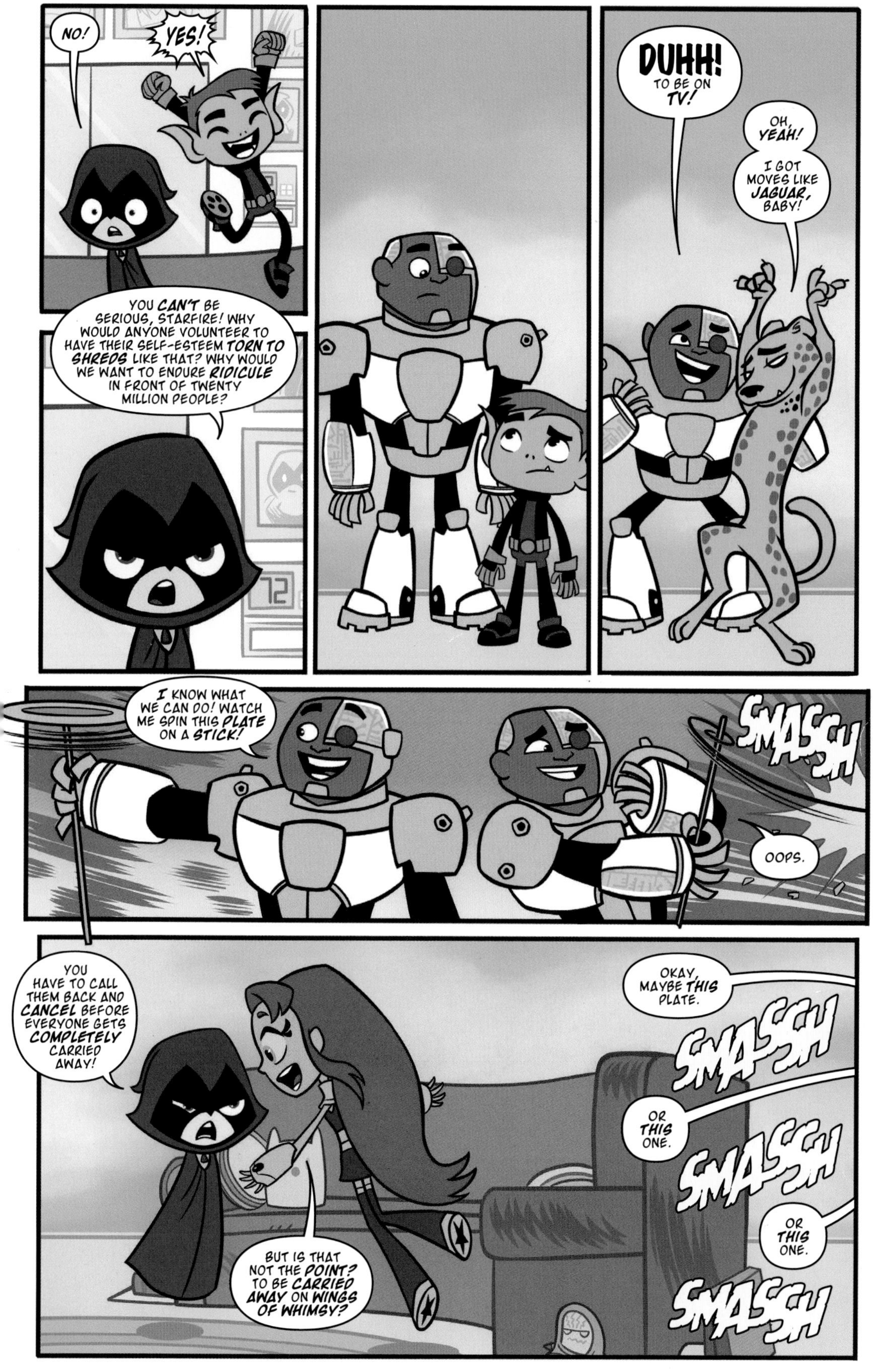

NO!
YES!
YOU CAN'T BE SERIOUS, STARFIRE! WHY WOULD ANYONE VOLUNTEER TO HAVE THEIR SELF-ESTEEM TORN TO SHREDS LIKE THAT? WHY WOULD WE WANT TO ENDURE RIDICULE IN FRONT OF TWENTY MILLION PEOPLE?
DUHH! TO BE ON TV!
OH, YEAH!
I GOT MOVES LIKE JAGUAR, BABY!
I KNOW WHAT WE CAN DO! WATCH ME SPIN THIS PLATE ON A STICK!
SMASCH
OOPS.
YOU HAVE TO CALL THEM BACK AND CANCEL BEFORE EVERYONE GETS COMPLETELY CARRIED AWAY!
OKAY, MAYBE THIS PLATE.
SMASCH
OR THIS ONE.
SMASCH
OR THIS ONE.
BUT IS THAT NOT THE POINT? TO BE CARRIED AWAY ON WINGS OF WHIMSY?
SMASCH

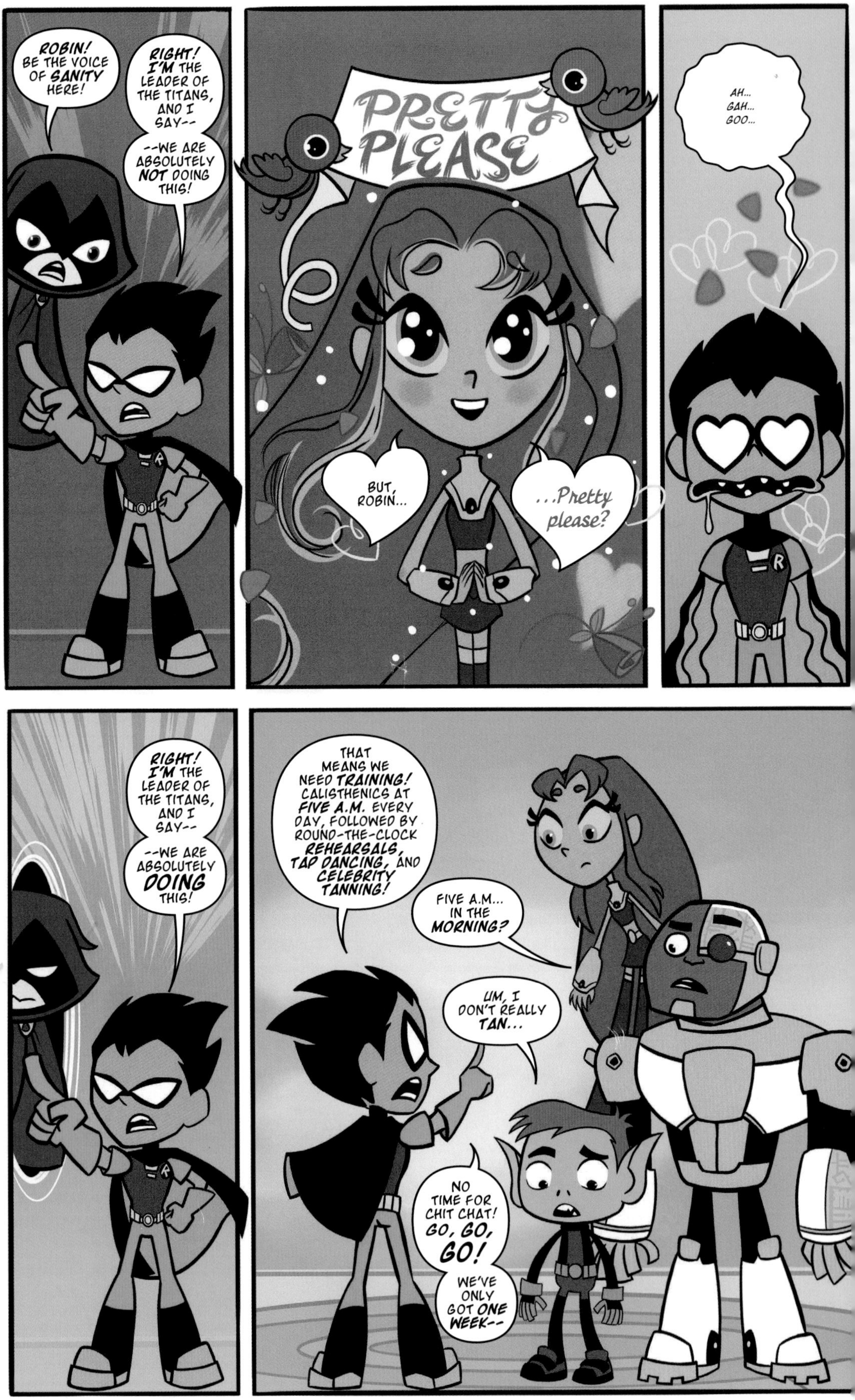
ROBIN! BE THE VOICE OF SANITY HERE!
RIGHT! I'M THE LEADER OF THE TITANS, AND I SAY--
--WE ARE ABSOLUTELY NOT DOING THIS!
PRETTY PLEASE
BUT, ROBIN...
...Pretty please?
AH... GAH... GOO...
RIGHT! I'M THE LEADER OF THE TITANS, AND I SAY--
--WE ARE ABSOLUTELY DOING THIS!
THAT MEANS WE NEED TRAINING! CALISTHENICS AT FIVE A.M. EVERY DAY, FOLLOWED BY ROUND-THE-CLOCK REHEARSALS, TAP DANCING, AND CELEBRITY TANNING!
FIVE A.M... IN THE MORNING?
UM, I DON'T REALLY TAN...
NO TIME FOR CHIT CHAT! GO, GO, GO!
WE'VE ONLY GOT ONE WEEK--

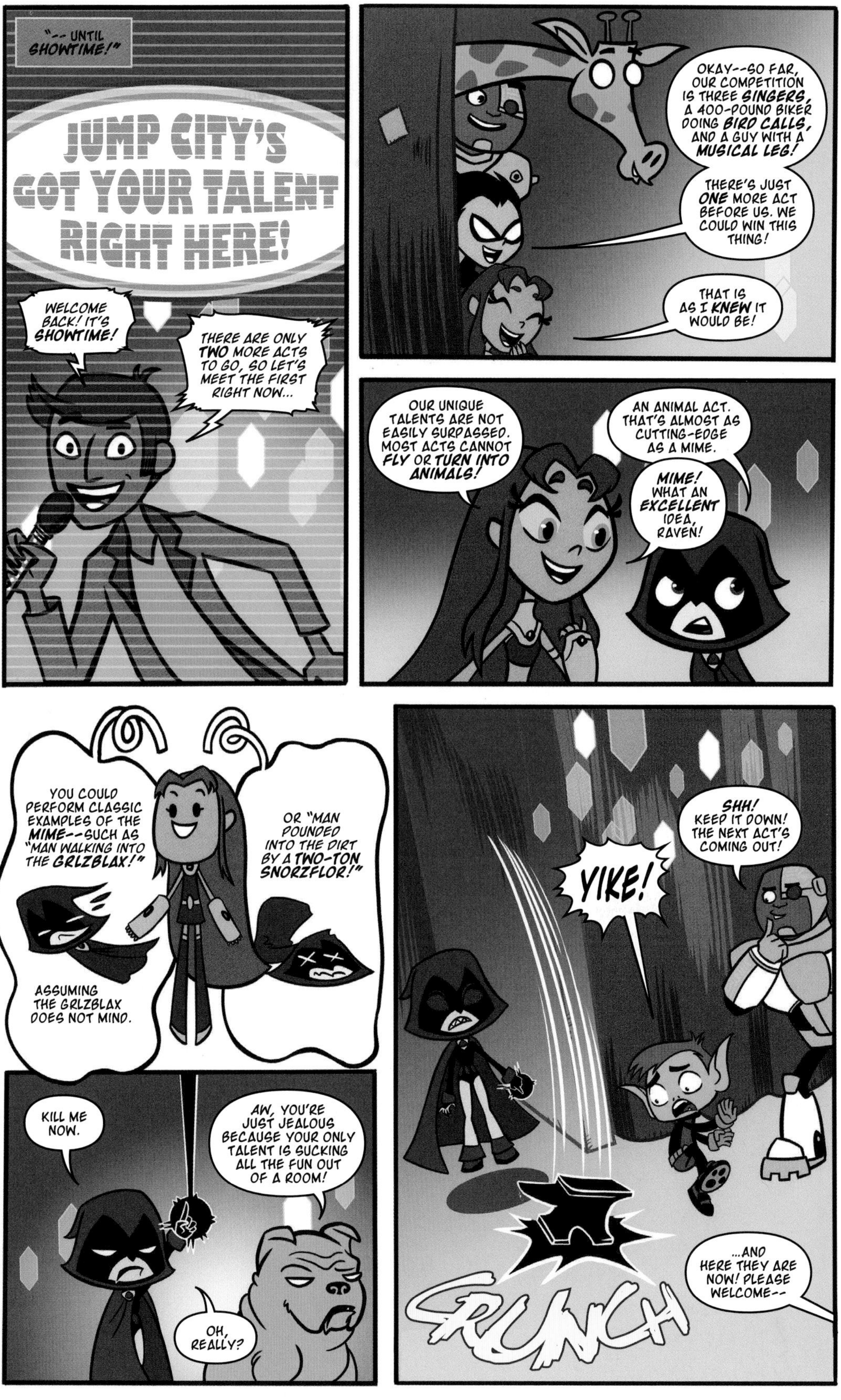
"-- UNTIL SHOWTIME!"
JUMP CITY'S GOT YOUR TALENT RIGHT HERE!
WELCOME BACK! IT'S SHOWTIME!
THERE ARE ONLY TWO MORE ACTS TO GO, SO LET'S MEET THE FIRST RIGHT NOW...
OKAY--SO FAR, OUR COMPETITION IS THREE SINGERS, A 400-POUND BIKER DOING BIRD CALLS, AND A GUY WITH A MUSICAL LEG!
THERE'S JUST ONE MORE ACT BEFORE US. WE COULD WIN THIS THING!
THAT IS AS I KNEW IT WOULD BE!
OUR UNIQUE TALENTS ARE NOT EASILY SURPASSED. MOST ACTS CANNOT FLY OR TURN INTO ANIMALS!
AN ANIMAL ACT. THAT'S ALMOST AS CUTTING-EDGE AS A MIME.
MIME! WHAT AN EXCELLENT IDEA, RAVEN!
YOU COULD PERFORM CLASSIC EXAMPLES OF THE MIME--SUCH AS "MAN WALKING INTO THE GRLZBLAX!"
OR "MAN POUNDED INTO THE DIRT BY A TWO-TON SNORZFLOR!"
ASSUMING THE GRLZBLAX DOES NOT MIND.
KILL ME NOW.
AW, YOU'RE JUST JEALOUS BECAUSE YOUR ONLY TALENT IS SUCKING ALL THE FUN OUT OF A ROOM!
OH, REALLY?
SHH! KEEP IT DOWN! THE NEXT ACT'S COMING OUT!
YIKE!
CRUNCH
...AND HERE THEY ARE NOW! PLEASE WELCOME--

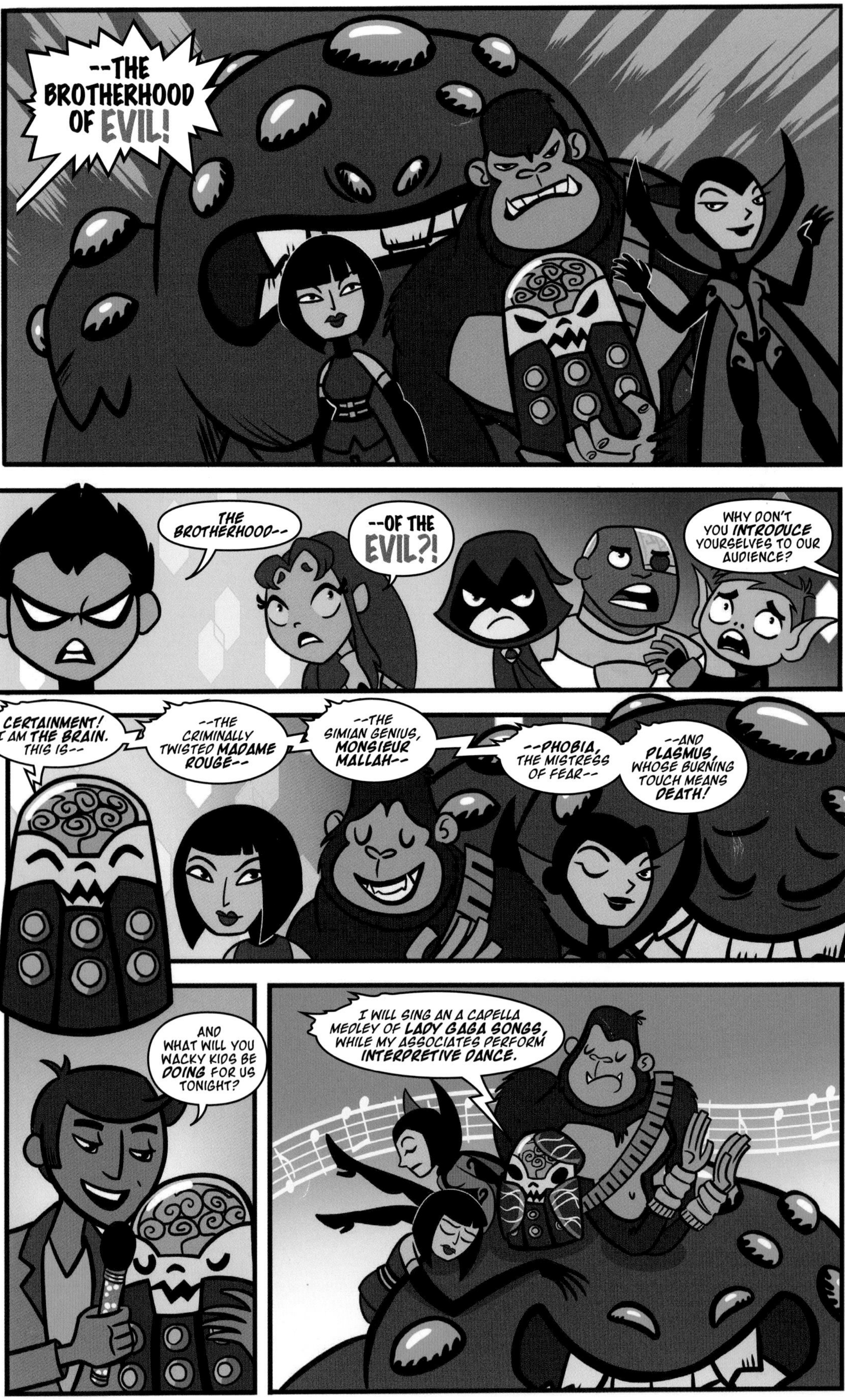
--THE BROTHERHOOD OF EVIL!
THE BROTHERHOOD--
--OF THE EVIL?!
WHY DON'T YOU INTRODUCE YOURSELVES TO OUR AUDIENCE?
CERTAINMENT! I AM THE BRAIN. THIS IS--
--THE CRIMINALLY TWISTED MADAME ROUGE--
--THE SIMIAN GENIUS, MONSIEUR MALLAH--
--PHOBIA, THE MISTRESS OF FEAR--
--AND PLASMUS, WHOSE BURNING TOUCH MEANS DEATH!
AND WHAT WILL YOU WACKY KIDS BE DOING FOR US TONIGHT?
I WILL SING AN A CAPELLA MEDLEY OF LADY GAGA SONGS, WHILE MY ASSOCIATES PERFORM INTERPRETIVE DANCE.

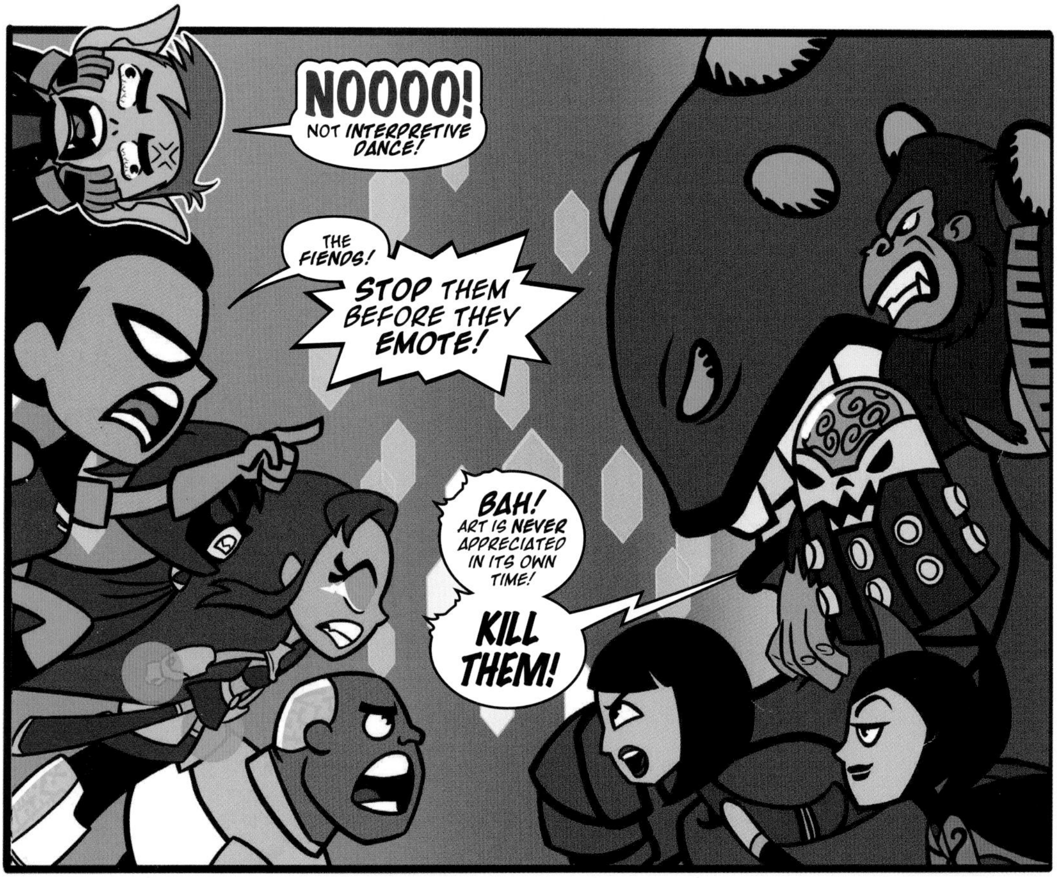
NOOOO!
NOT INTERPRETIVE DANCE!
THE FIENDS!
STOP THEM BEFORE THEY EMOTE!
BAH! ART IS NEVER APPRECIATED IN ITS OWN TIME!
KILL THEM!

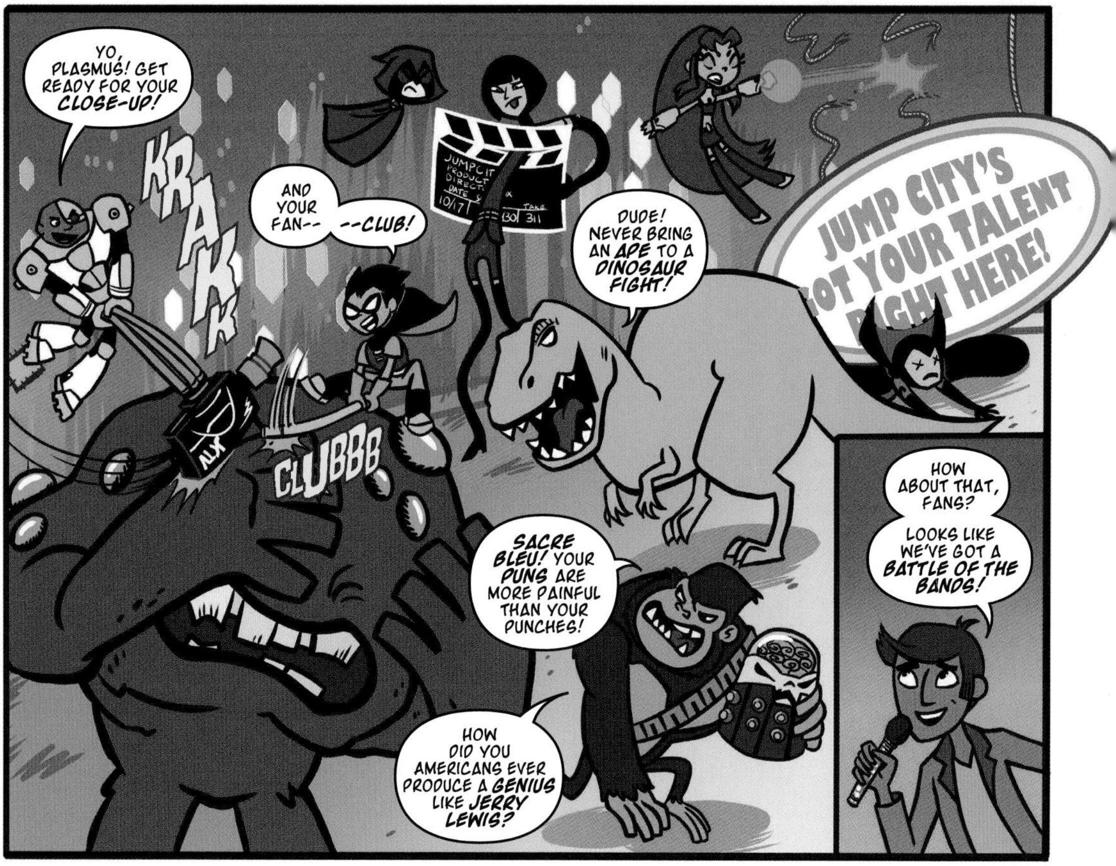
YO, PLASMUS! GET READY FOR YOUR CLOSE-UP!
KRAKK
AND YOUR FAN--
--CLUB!
JUMP CITY
DUDE! NEVER BRING AN APE TO A DINOSAUR FIGHT!
JUMP CITY'S GOT YOUR TALENT RIGHT HERE!
CLUBBB
SACRE BLEU! YOUR PUNS ARE MORE PAINFUL THAN YOUR PUNCHES!
HOW DID YOU AMERICANS EVER PRODUCE A GENIUS LIKE JERRY LEWIS?
HOW ABOUT THAT, FANS?
LOOKS LIKE WE'VE GOT A BATTLE OF THE BANDS!

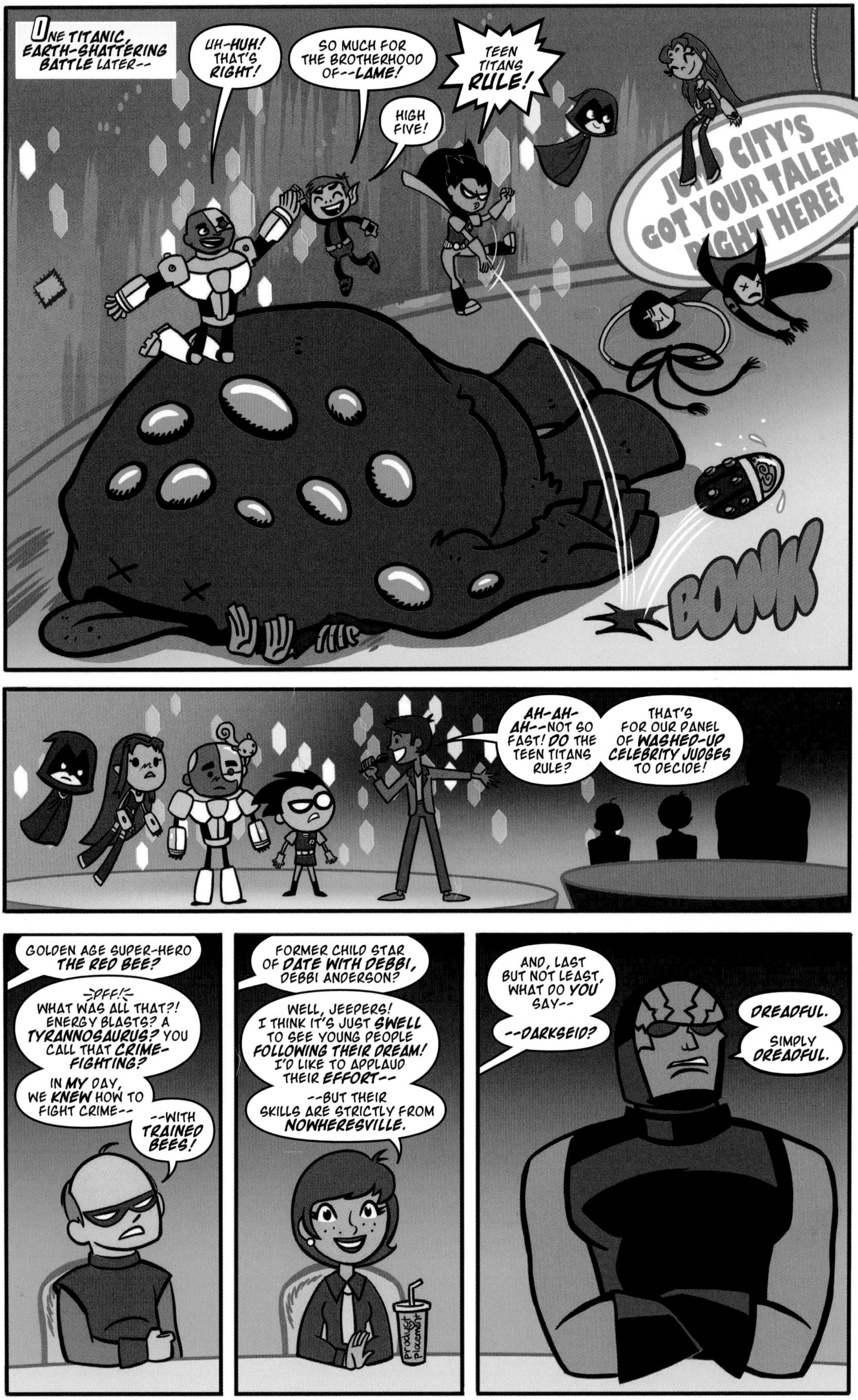

ONE TITANIC, EARTH-SHATTERING BATTLE LATER--
UH-HUH! THAT'S RIGHT!
SO MUCH FOR THE BROTHERHOOD OF--LAME!
HIGH FIVE!
TEEN TITANS RULE!
CITY'S
GOT YOUR TALENT
HERE!
BONK
AH-AH-AH--NOT SO FAST! DO THE TEEN TITANS RULE?
THAT'S FOR OUR PANEL OF WASHED-UP CELEBRITY JUDGES TO DECIDE!
GOLDEN AGE SUPER-HERO THE RED BEE?
PFF! WHAT WAS ALL THAT?! ENERGY BLASTS? A TYRANNOSAURUS? YOU CALL THAT CRIME-FIGHTING?
IN MY DAY, WE KNEW HOW TO FIGHT CRIME--
--WITH TRAINED BEES!
FORMER CHILD STAR OF DATE WITH DEBBI, DEBBI ANDERSON?
WELL, JEEPERS! I THINK IT'S JUST SWELL TO SEE YOUNG PEOPLE FOLLOWING THEIR DREAM! I'D LIKE TO APPLAUD THEIR EFFORT--
--BUT THEIR SKILLS ARE STRICTLY FROM NOWHERESVILLE.
product placement
AND, LAST BUT NOT LEAST, WHAT DO YOU SAY--
--DARKSEID?
DREADFUL.
SIMPLY DREADFUL.

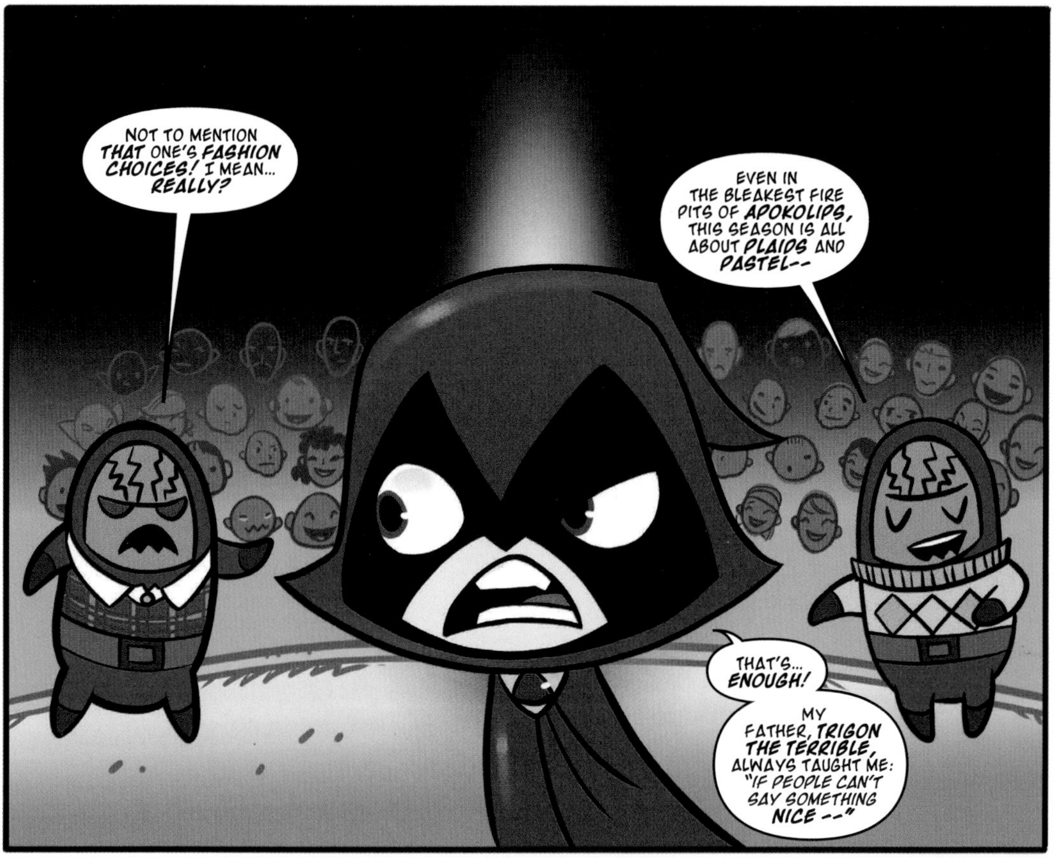
NOT TO MENTION THAT ONE'S FASHION CHOICES! I MEAN... REALLY?
EVEN IN THE BLEAKEST FIRE PITS OF APOKOLIPS, THIS SEASON IS ALL ABOUT PLAIDS AND PASTEL--
THAT'S... ENOUGH!
MY FATHER, TRIGON THE TERRIBLE, ALWAYS TAUGHT ME: "IF PEOPLE CAN'T SAY SOMETHING NICE --"

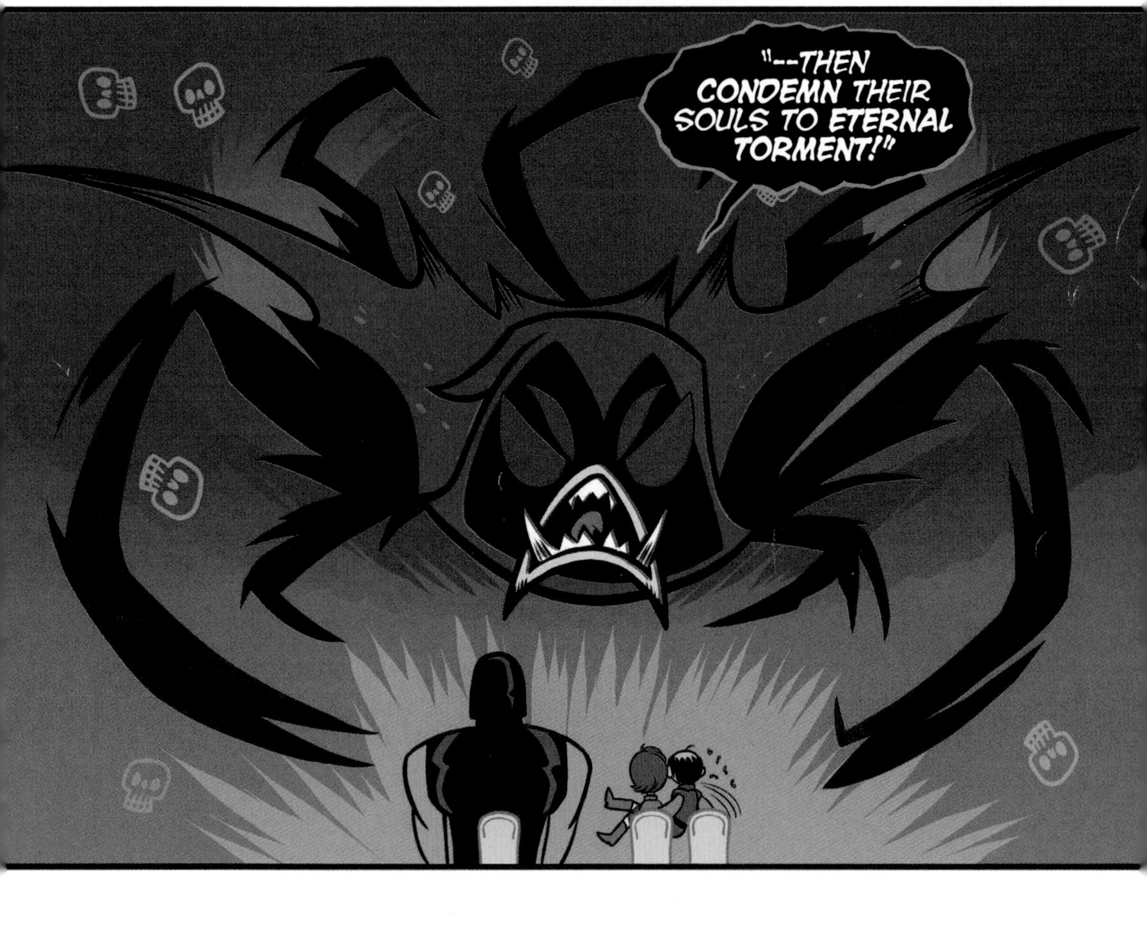
"--THEN CONDEMN THEIR SOULS TO ETERNAL TORMENT!"

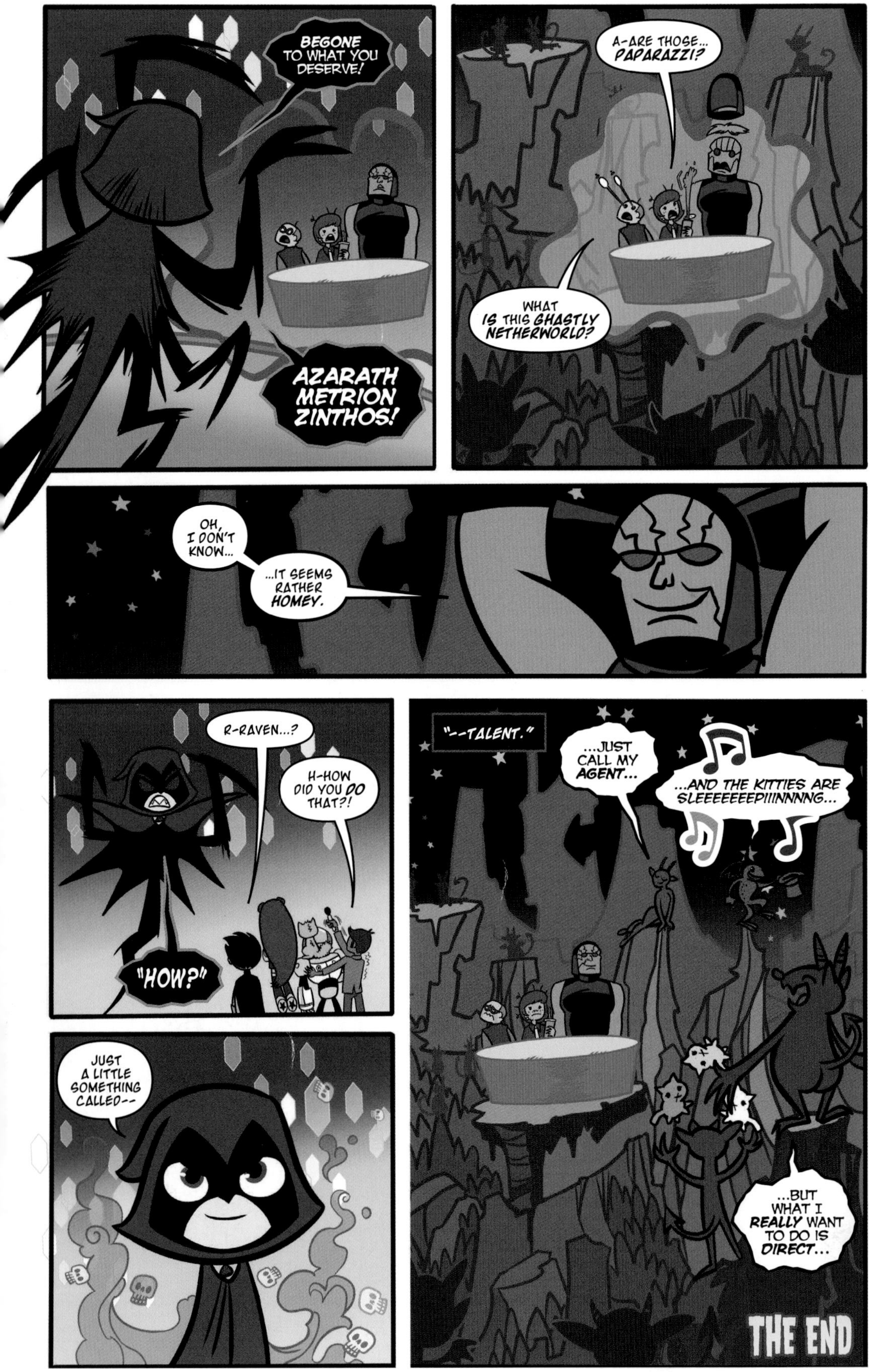
BEGONE TO WHAT YOU DESERVE!
AZARATH METRION ZINTHOS!
A-ARE THOSE... PAPARAZZI?
WHAT IS THIS GHASTLY NETHERWORLD?
OH, I DON'T KNOW...
...IT SEEMS RATHER HOMEY.
R-RAVEN...?
H-HOW DID YOU DO THAT?!
"HOW?"
JUST A LITTLE SOMETHING CALLED--
"--TALENT."
...JUST CALL MY AGENT...
...AND THE KITTIES ARE SLEEEEEEEPIIINNNNG...
...BUT WHAT I REALLY WANT TO DO IS DIRECT...
THE END

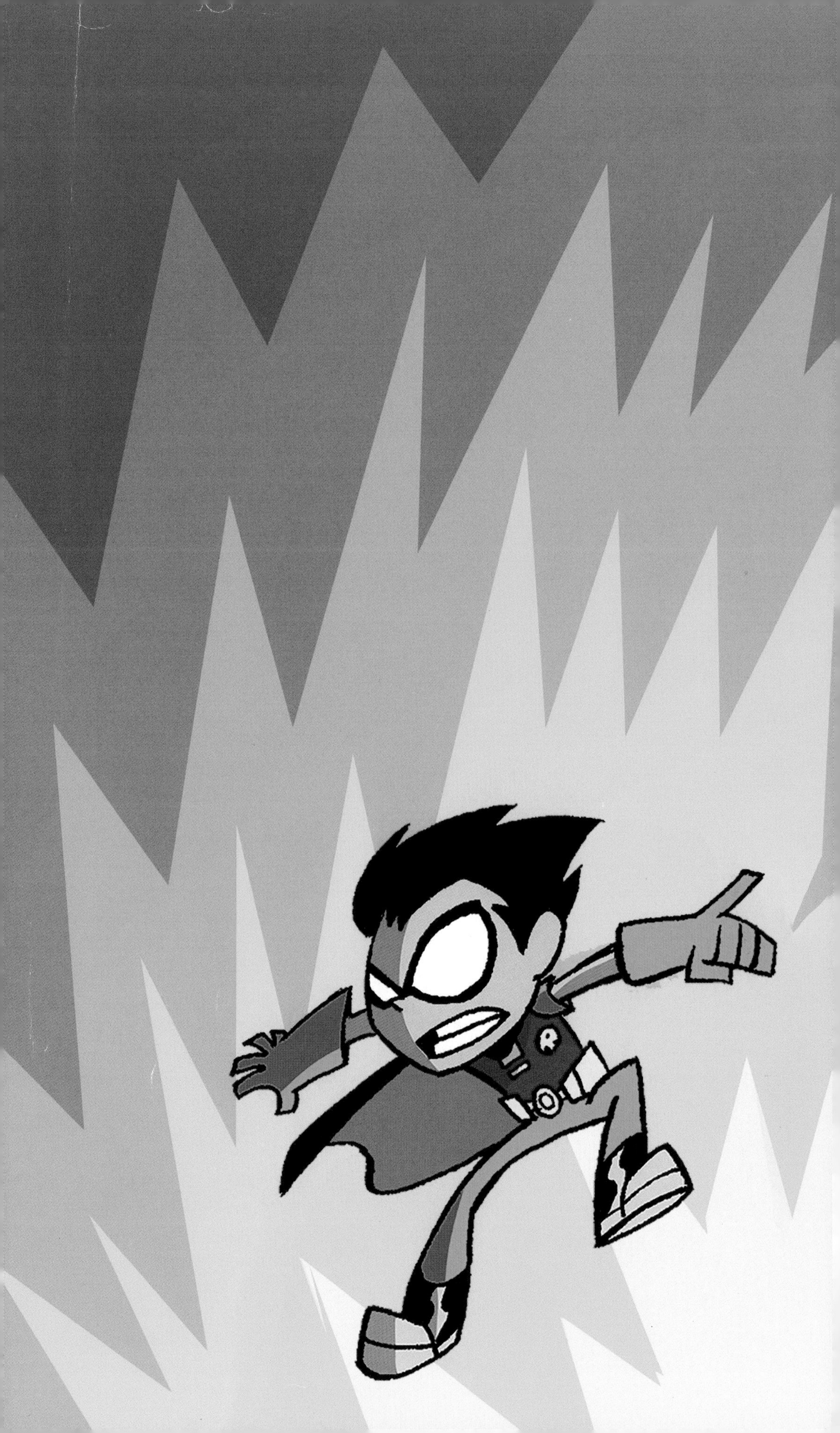

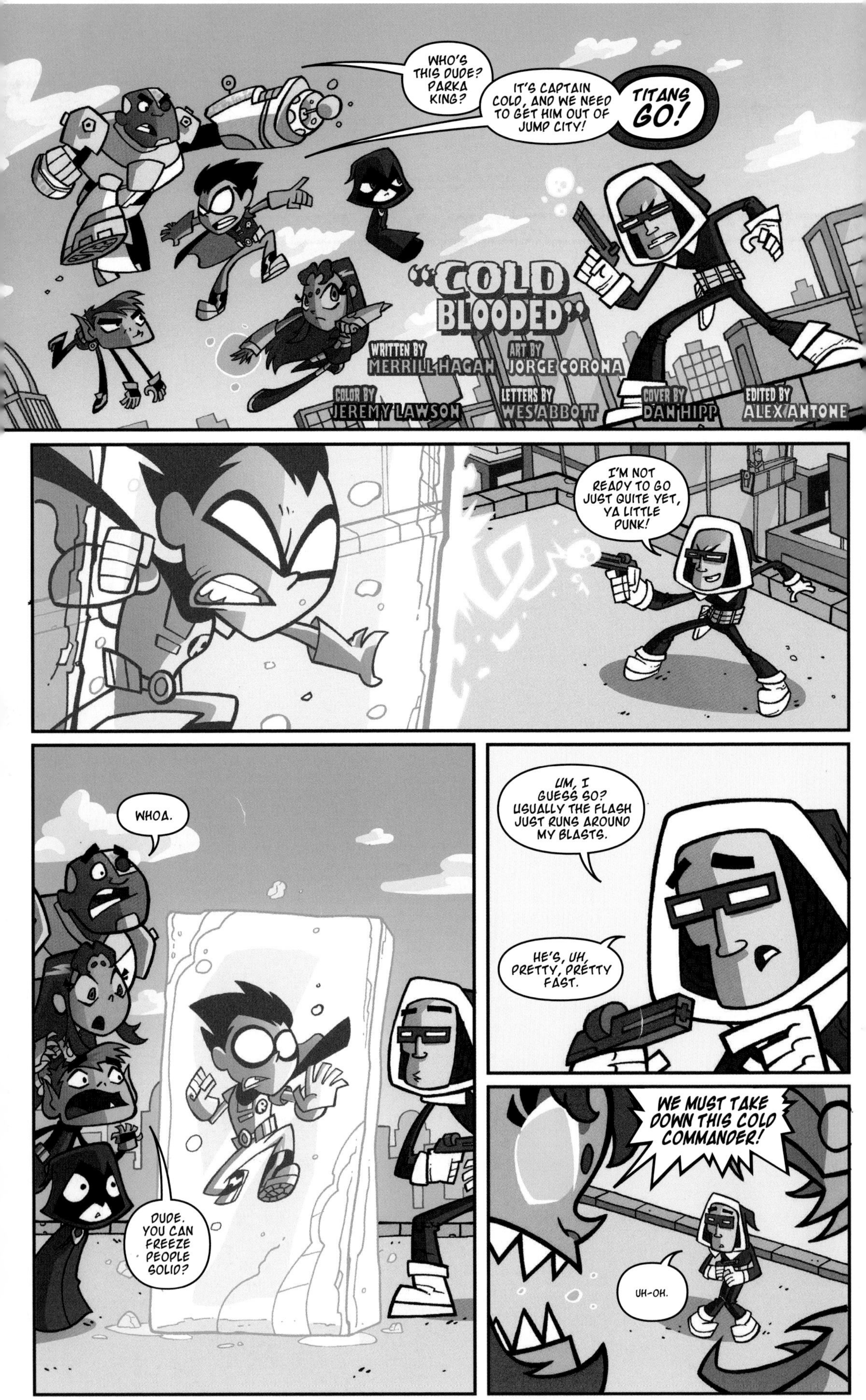
WHO'S THIS DUDE? PARKA KING?
IT'S CAPTAIN COLD, AND WE NEED TO GET HIM OUT OF JUMP CITY!
TITANS GO!
"COLD BLOODED"
WRITTEN BY MERRILL HAGAN
ART BY JORGE CORONA
COLOR BY JEREMY LAWSON
LETTERS BY WES ABBOTT
COVER BY DAN HIPP
EDITED BY ALEX ANTONE
I'M NOT READY TO GO JUST QUITE YET, YA LITTLE PUNK!
WHOA.
DUDE. YOU CAN FREEZE PEOPLE SOLID?
UM, I GUESS SO? USUALLY THE FLASH JUST RUNS AROUND MY BLASTS.
HE'S, UH, PRETTY, PRETTY FAST.
WE MUST TAKE DOWN THIS COLD COMMANDER!
UH-OH.

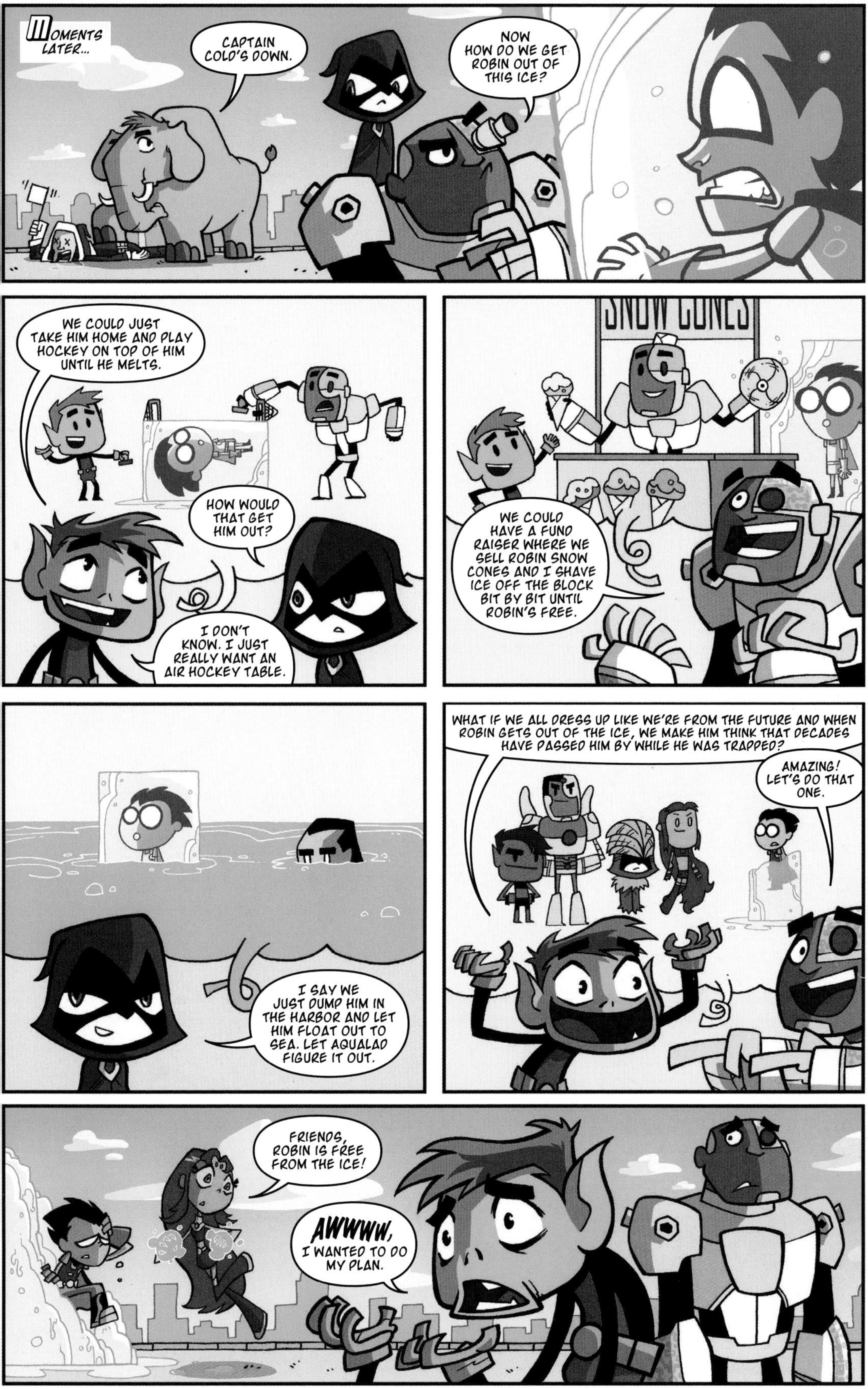
MOMENTS LATER...
CAPTAIN COLD'S DOWN.
NOW HOW DO WE GET ROBIN OUT OF THIS ICE?
WE COULD JUST TAKE HIM HOME AND PLAY HOCKEY ON TOP OF HIM UNTIL HE MELTS.
HOW WOULD THAT GET HIM OUT?
I DON'T KNOW. I JUST REALLY WANT AN AIR HOCKEY TABLE.
SNOW CONES
WE COULD HAVE A FUND RAISER WHERE WE SELL ROBIN SNOW CONES AND I SHAVE ICE OFF THE BLOCK BIT BY BIT UNTIL ROBIN'S FREE.
I SAY WE JUST DUMP HIM IN THE HARBOR AND LET HIM FLOAT OUT TO SEA. LET AQUALAD FIGURE IT OUT.
WHAT IF WE ALL DRESS UP LIKE WE'RE FROM THE FUTURE AND WHEN ROBIN GETS OUT OF THE ICE, WE MAKE HIM THINK THAT DECADES HAVE PASSED HIM BY WHILE HE WAS TRAPPED?
AMAZING! LET'S DO THAT ONE.
FRIENDS, ROBIN IS FREE FROM THE ICE!
AWWWW, I WANTED TO DO MY PLAN.

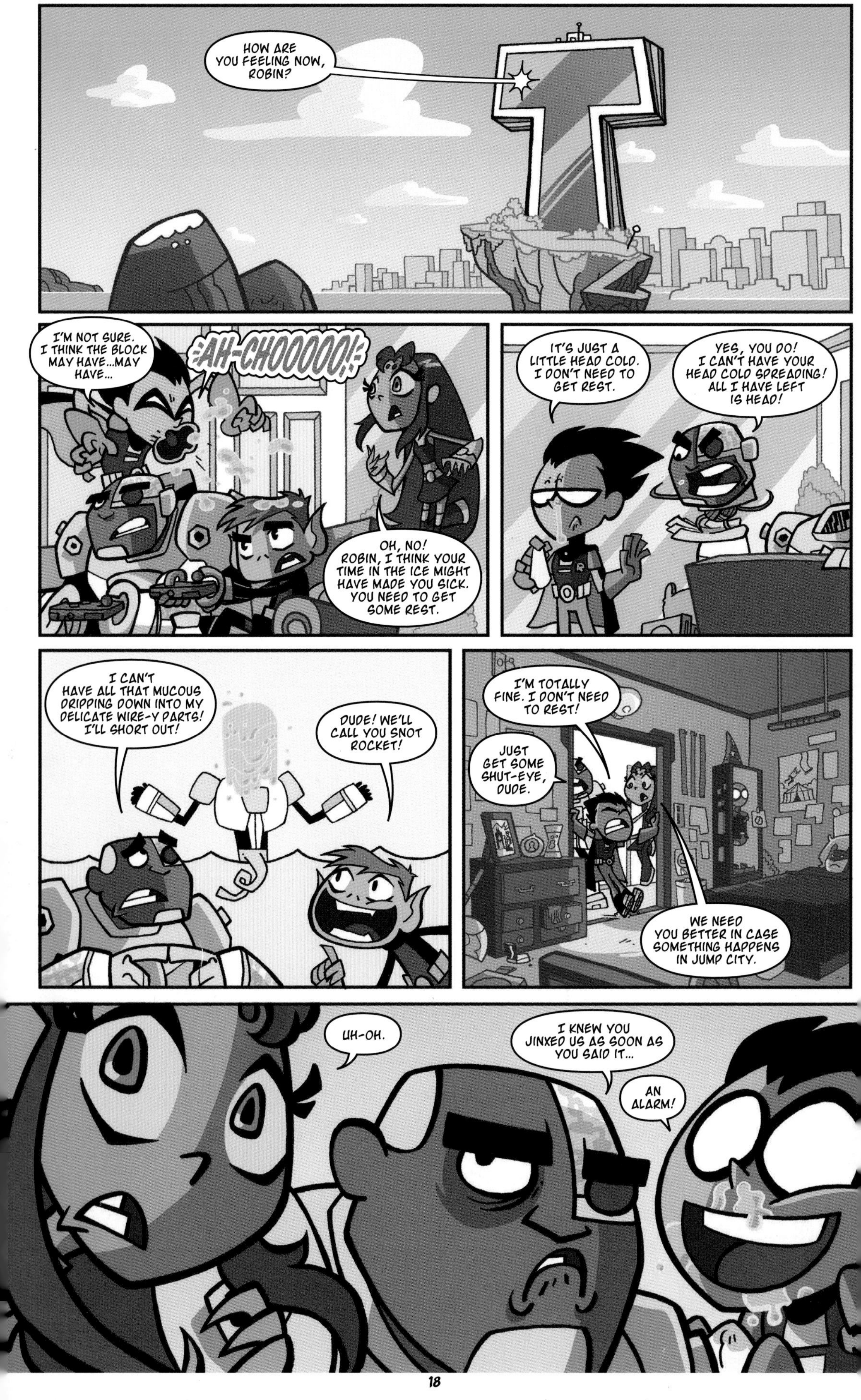
HOW ARE YOU FEELING NOW, ROBIN?
I'M NOT SURE. I THINK THE BLOCK MAY HAVE...MAY HAVE...
AH-CHOOOOO!
OH, NO! ROBIN, I THINK YOUR TIME IN THE ICE MIGHT HAVE MADE YOU SICK. YOU NEED TO GET SOME REST.
IT'S JUST A LITTLE HEAD COLD. I DON'T NEED TO GET REST.
YES, YOU DO! I CAN'T HAVE YOUR HEAD COLD SPREADING! ALL I HAVE LEFT IS HEAD!
I CAN'T HAVE ALL THAT MUCOUS DRIPPING DOWN INTO MY DELICATE WIRE-Y PARTS! I'LL SHORT OUT!
DUDE! WE'LL CALL YOU SNOT ROCKET!
I'M TOTALLY FINE. I DON'T NEED TO REST!
JUST GET SOME SHUT-EYE, DUDE.
WE NEED YOU BETTER IN CASE SOMETHING HAPPENS IN JUMP CITY.
UH-OH.
I KNEW YOU JINXED US AS SOON AS YOU SAID IT...
AN ALARM!

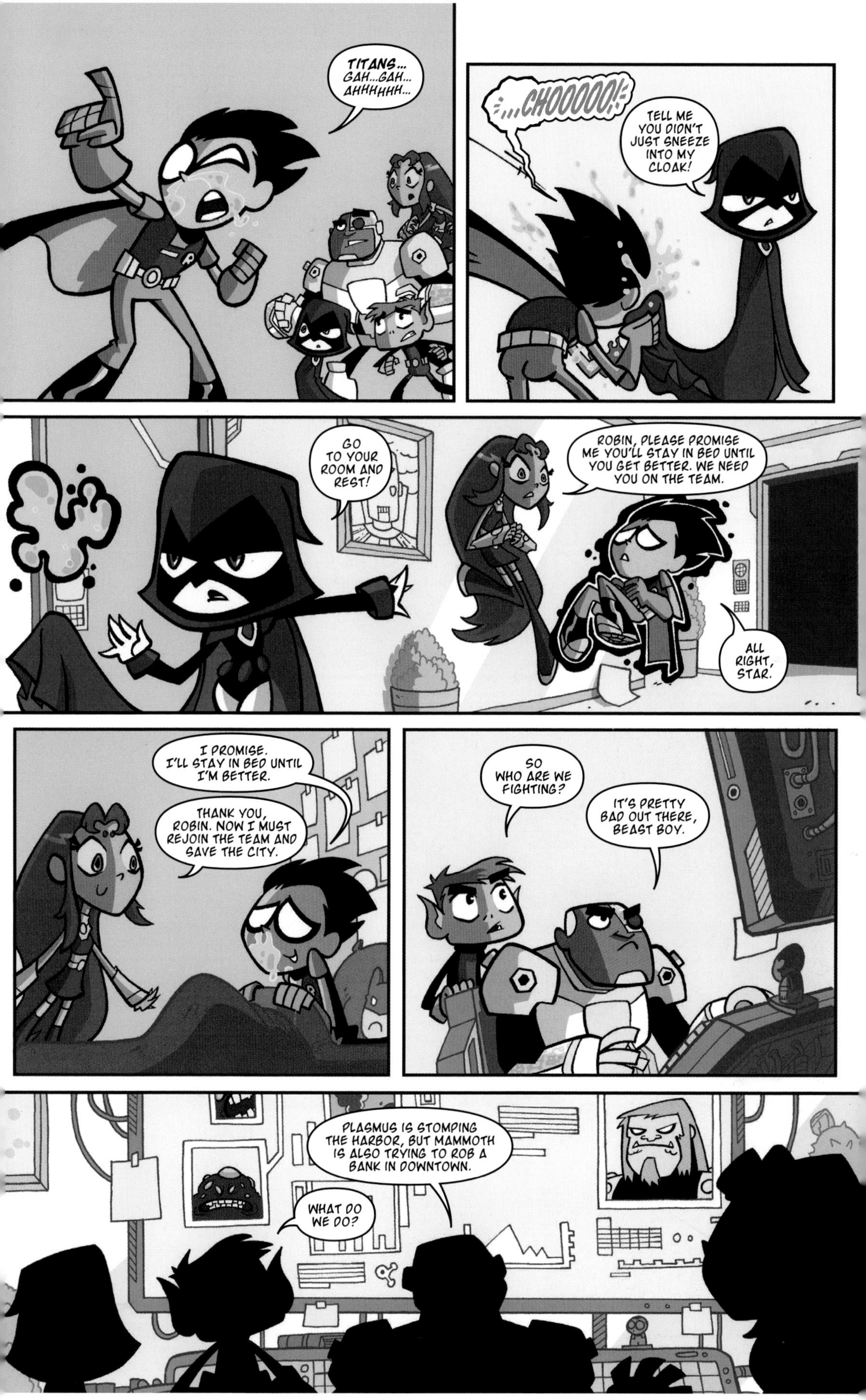
TITANS... GAH...GAH... AHHHHHH...
,,,,CHOOOOO!
TELL ME YOU DIDN'T JUST SNEEZE INTO MY CLOAK!
GO TO YOUR ROOM AND REST!
ROBIN, PLEASE PROMISE ME YOU'LL STAY IN BED UNTIL YOU GET BETTER. WE NEED YOU ON THE TEAM.
ALL RIGHT, STAR.
I PROMISE. I'LL STAY IN BED UNTIL I'M BETTER.
THANK YOU, ROBIN. NOW I MUST REJOIN THE TEAM AND SAVE THE CITY.
SO WHO ARE WE FIGHTING?
IT'S PRETTY BAD OUT THERE, BEAST BOY.
PLASMUS IS STOMPING THE HARBOR, BUT MAMMOTH IS ALSO TRYING TO ROB A BANK IN DOWNTOWN.
WHAT DO WE DO?

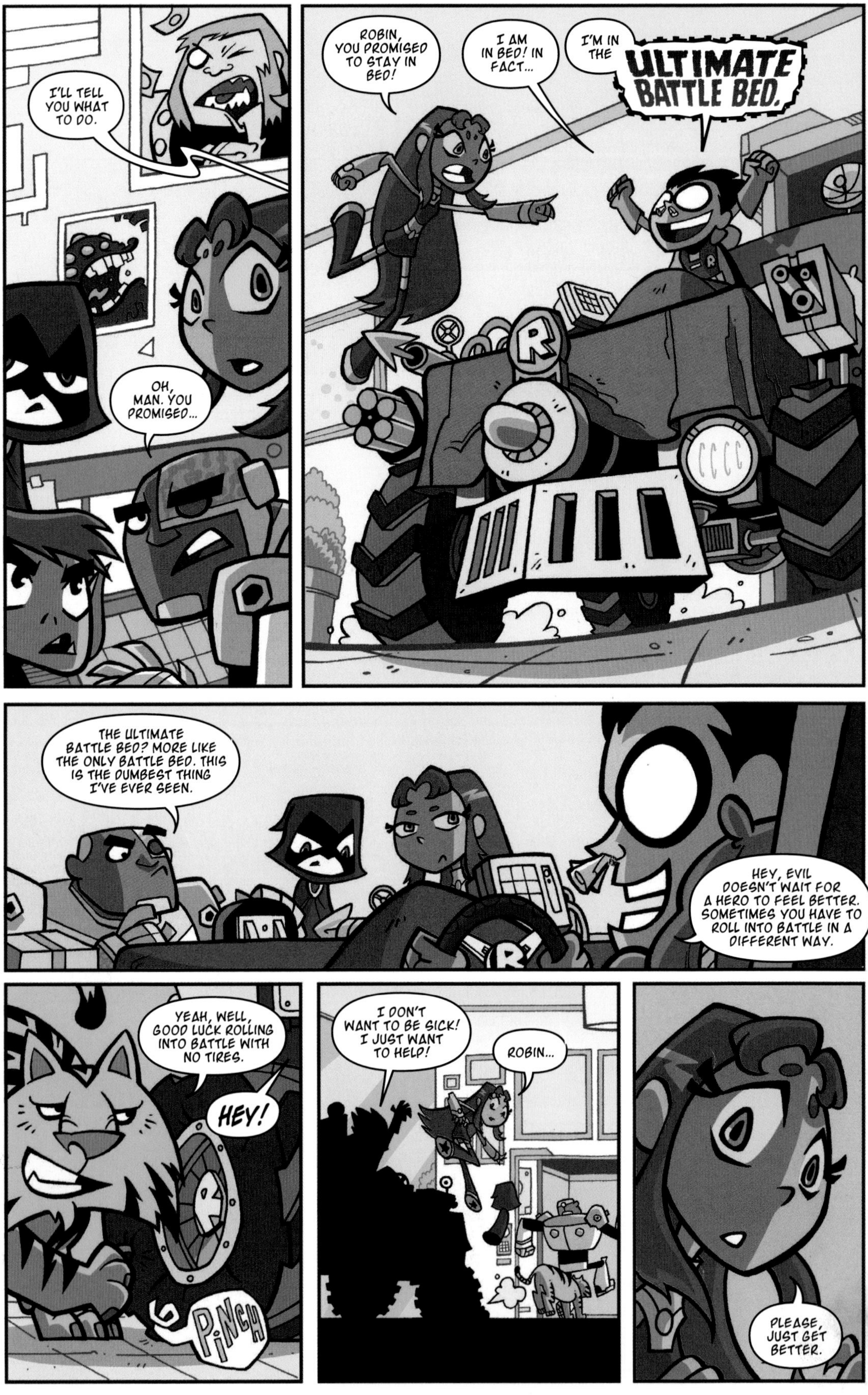

I'LL TELL YOU WHAT TO DO.
OH, MAN. YOU PROMISED...
ROBIN, YOU PROMISED TO STAY IN BED!
I AM IN BED! IN FACT...
I'M IN THE
ULTIMATE BATTLE BED.
THE ULTIMATE BATTLE BED? MORE LIKE THE ONLY BATTLE BED. THIS IS THE DUMBEST THING I'VE EVER SEEN.
HEY, EVIL DOESN'T WAIT FOR A HERO TO FEEL BETTER. SOMETIMES YOU HAVE TO ROLL INTO BATTLE IN A DIFFERENT WAY.
YEAH, WELL, GOOD LUCK ROLLING INTO BATTLE WITH NO TIRES.
HEY!
PINCH
I DON'T WANT TO BE SICK! I JUST WANT TO HELP!
ROBIN...
PLEASE, JUST GET BETTER.

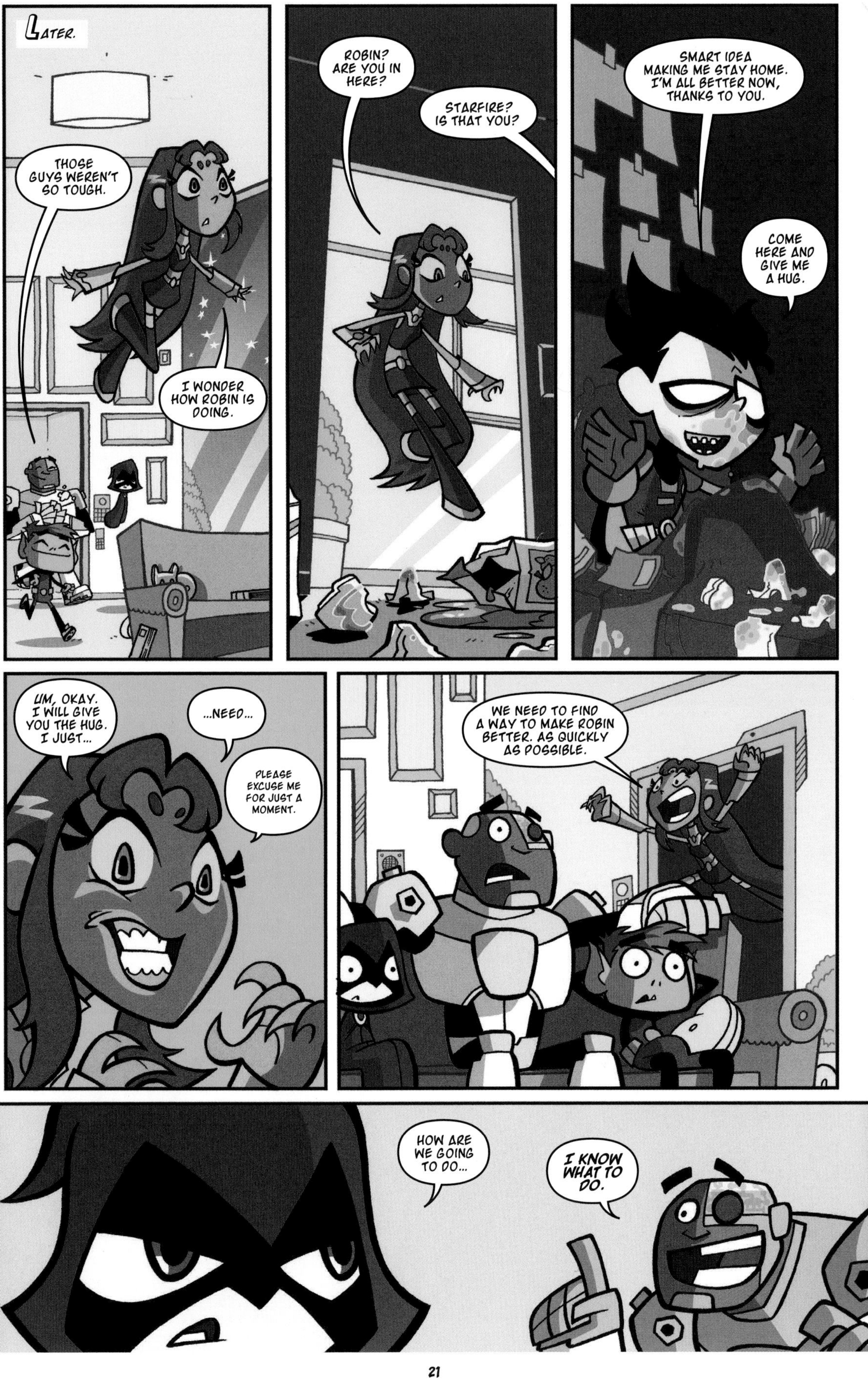
Later.
THOSE GUYS WEREN'T SO TOUGH.
I WONDER HOW ROBIN IS DOING.
ROBIN? ARE YOU IN HERE?
STARFIRE? IS THAT YOU?
SMART IDEA MAKING ME STAY HOME. I'M ALL BETTER NOW, THANKS TO YOU.
COME HERE AND GIVE ME A HUG.
UM, OKAY. I WILL GIVE YOU THE HUG. I JUST...
...NEED...
PLEASE EXCUSE ME FOR JUST A MOMENT.
WE NEED TO FIND A WAY TO MAKE ROBIN BETTER. AS QUICKLY AS POSSIBLE.
HOW ARE WE GOING TO DO...
I KNOW WHAT TO DO.

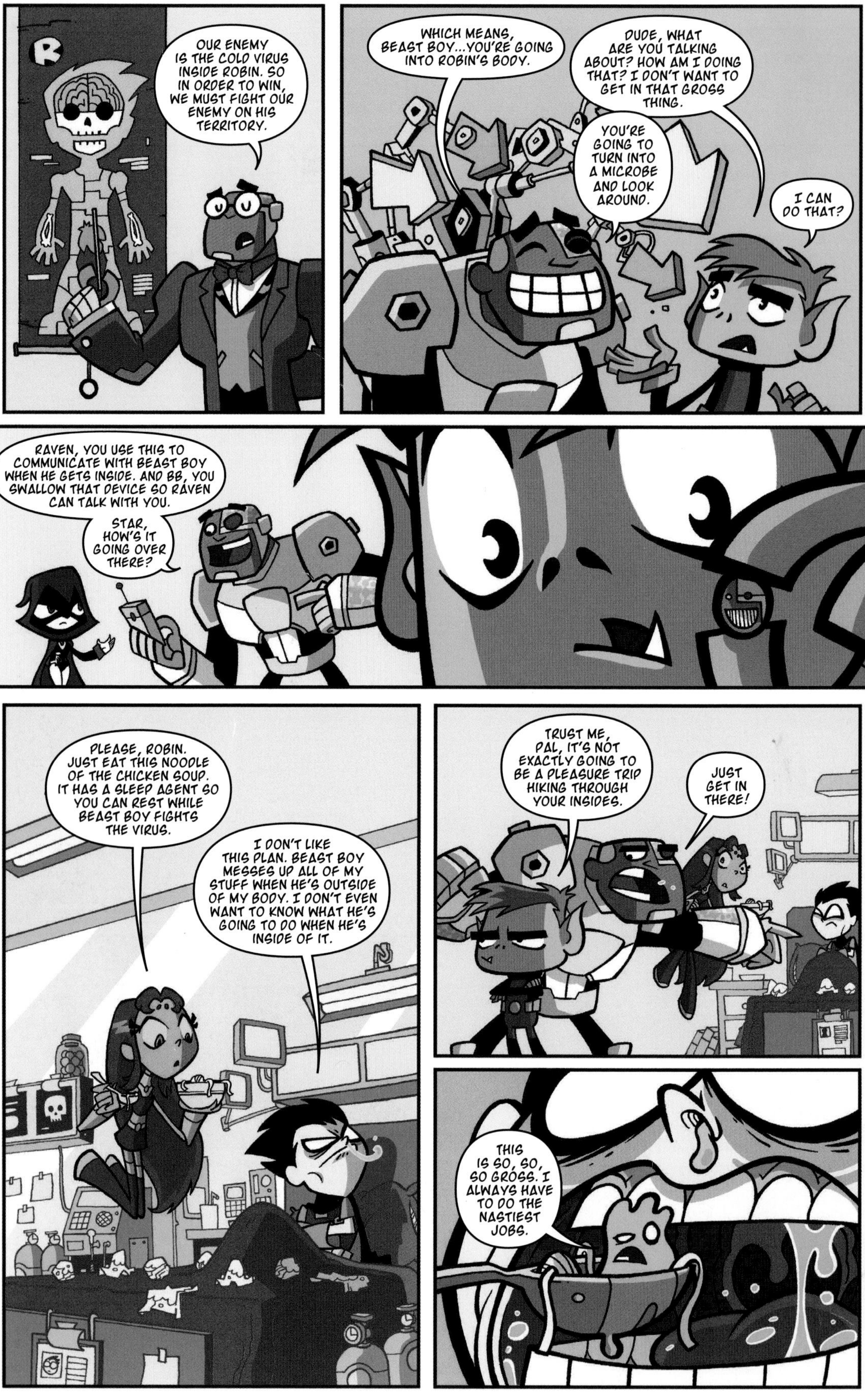
OUR ENEMY IS THE COLD VIRUS INSIDE ROBIN. SO IN ORDER TO WIN, WE MUST FIGHT OUR ENEMY ON HIS TERRITORY.
WHICH MEANS, BEAST BOY...YOU'RE GOING INTO ROBIN'S BODY.
DUDE, WHAT ARE YOU TALKING ABOUT? HOW AM I DOING THAT? I DON'T WANT TO GET IN THAT GROSS THING.
YOU'RE GOING TO TURN INTO A MICROBE AND LOOK AROUND.
I CAN DO THAT?
RAVEN, YOU USE THIS TO COMMUNICATE WITH BEAST BOY WHEN HE GETS INSIDE. AND BB, YOU SWALLOW THAT DEVICE SO RAVEN CAN TALK WITH YOU.
STAR, HOW'S IT GOING OVER THERE?
PLEASE, ROBIN. JUST EAT THIS NOODLE OF THE CHICKEN SOUP. IT HAS A SLEEP AGENT SO YOU CAN REST WHILE BEAST BOY FIGHTS THE VIRUS.
I DON'T LIKE THIS PLAN. BEAST BOY MESSES UP ALL OF MY STUFF WHEN HE'S OUTSIDE OF MY BODY. I DON'T EVEN WANT TO KNOW WHAT HE'S GOING TO DO WHEN HE'S INSIDE OF IT.
TRUST ME, PAL, IT'S NOT EXACTLY GOING TO BE A PLEASURE TRIP HIKING THROUGH YOUR INSIDES.
JUST GET IN THERE!
THIS IS SO, SO, SO GROSS. I ALWAYS HAVE TO DO THE NASTIEST JOBS.

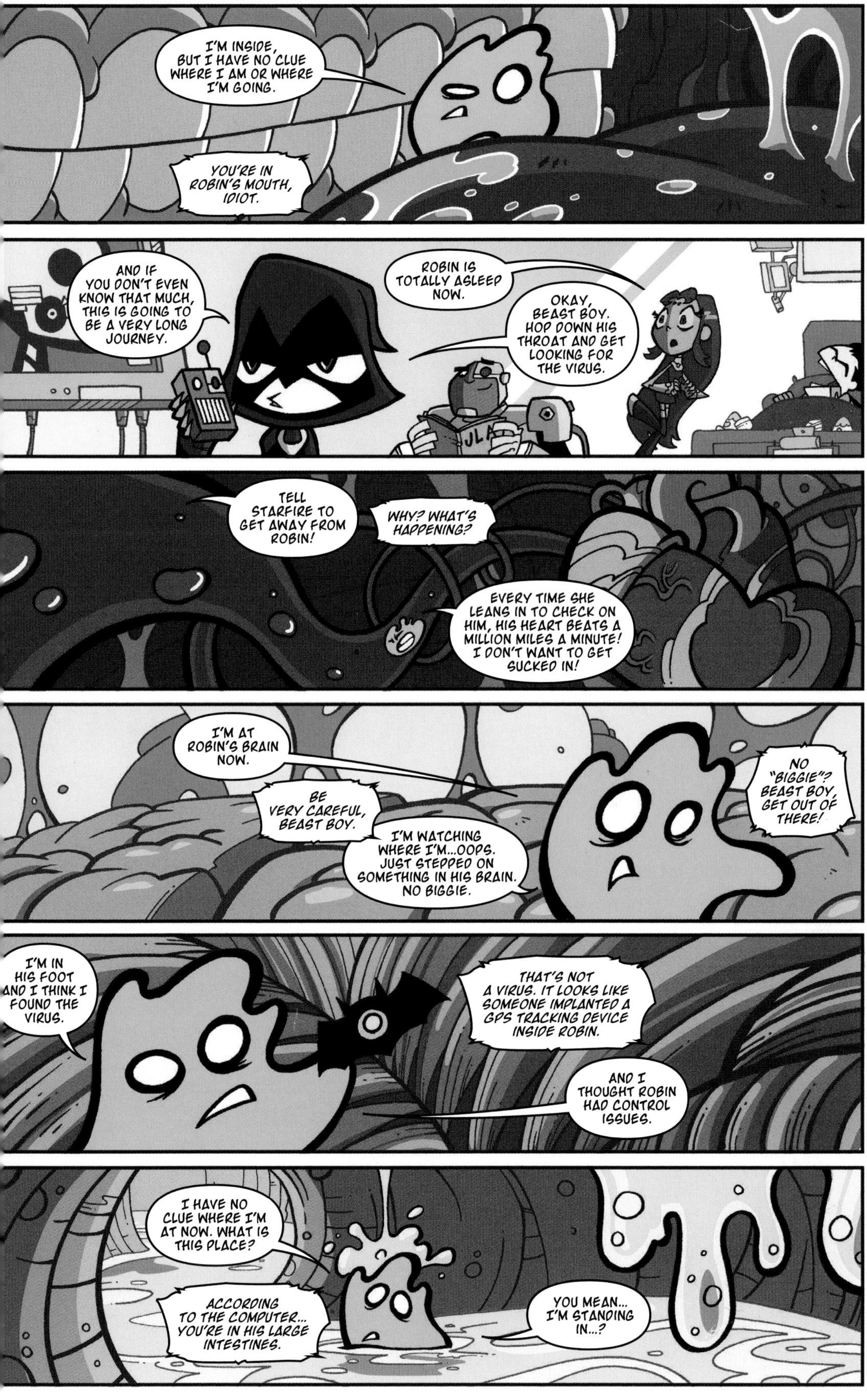

I'M INSIDE, BUT I HAVE NO CLUE WHERE I AM OR WHERE I'M GOING.
YOU'RE IN ROBIN'S MOUTH, IDIOT.
AND IF YOU DON'T EVEN KNOW THAT MUCH, THIS IS GOING TO BE A VERY LONG JOURNEY.
ROBIN IS TOTALLY ASLEEP NOW.
OKAY, BEAST BOY. HOP DOWN HIS THROAT AND GET LOOKING FOR THE VIRUS.
JLA
TELL STARFIRE TO GET AWAY FROM ROBIN!
WHY? WHAT'S HAPPENING?
EVERY TIME SHE LEANS IN TO CHECK ON HIM, HIS HEART BEATS A MILLION MILES A MINUTE! I DON'T WANT TO GET SUCKED IN!
I'M AT ROBIN'S BRAIN NOW.
BE VERY CAREFUL, BEAST BOY.
I'M WATCHING WHERE I'M...OOPS. JUST STEPPED ON SOMETHING IN HIS BRAIN. NO BIGGIE.
NO "BIGGIE"? BEAST BOY, GET OUT OF THERE!
I'M IN HIS FOOT AND I THINK I FOUND THE VIRUS.
THAT'S NOT A VIRUS. IT LOOKS LIKE SOMEONE IMPLANTED A GPS TRACKING DEVICE INSIDE ROBIN.
AND I THOUGHT ROBIN HAD CONTROL ISSUES.
I HAVE NO CLUE WHERE I'M AT NOW. WHAT IS THIS PLACE?
ACCORDING TO THE COMPUTER... YOU'RE IN HIS LARGE INTESTINES.
YOU MEAN... I'M STANDING IN...?

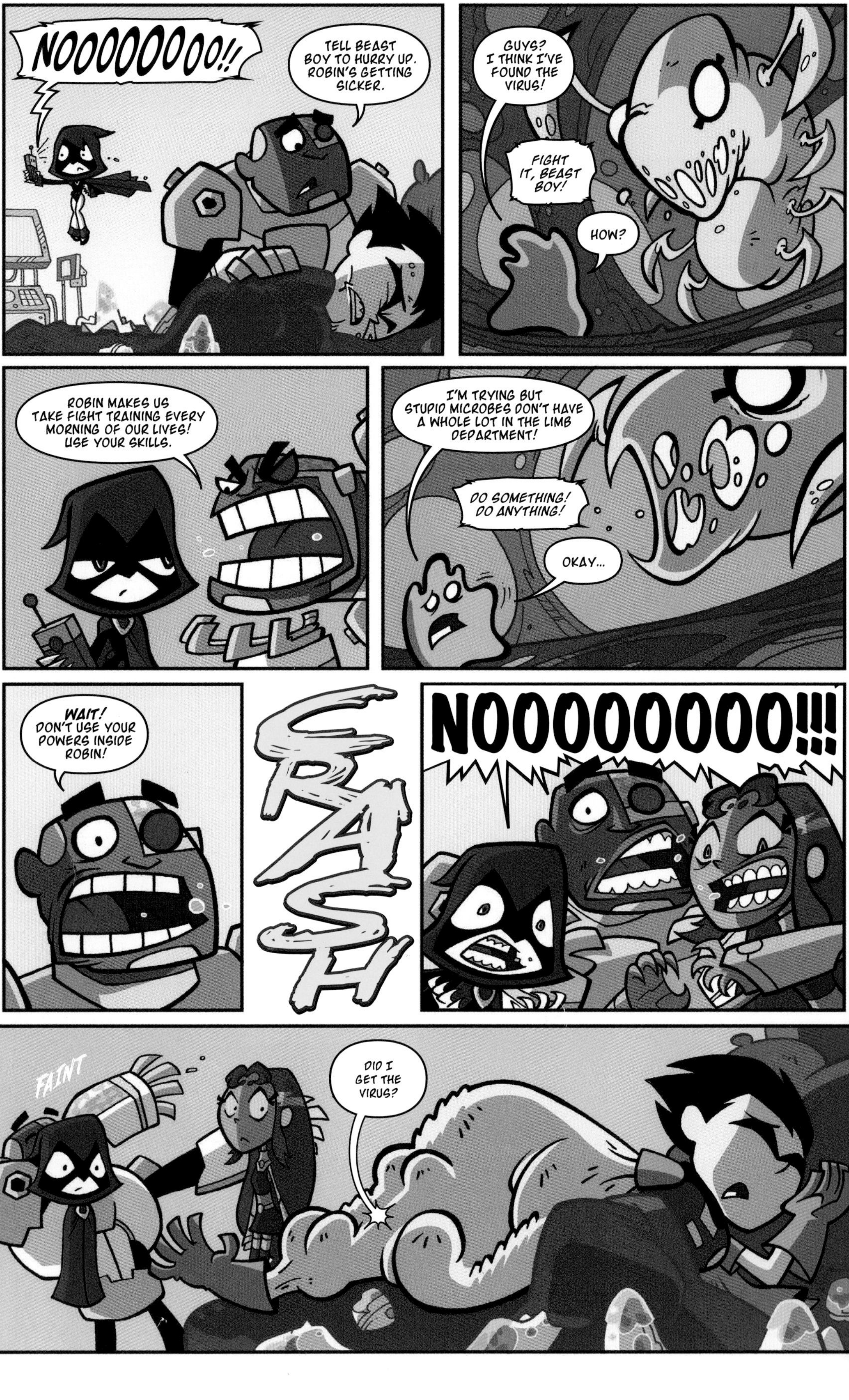
NOOOOOOOO!!
TELL BEAST BOY TO HURRY UP. ROBIN'S GETTING SICKER.
GUYS? I THINK I'VE FOUND THE VIRUS!
FIGHT IT, BEAST BOY!
HOW?
ROBIN MAKES US TAKE FIGHT TRAINING EVERY MORNING OF OUR LIVES! USE YOUR SKILLS.
I'M TRYING BUT STUPID MICROBES DON'T HAVE A WHOLE LOT IN THE LIMB DEPARTMENT!
DO SOMETHING! DO ANYTHING!
OKAY...
WAIT! DON'T USE YOUR POWERS INSIDE ROBIN!
CRASH
NOOOOOOOOO!!!
FAINT
DID I GET THE VIRUS?

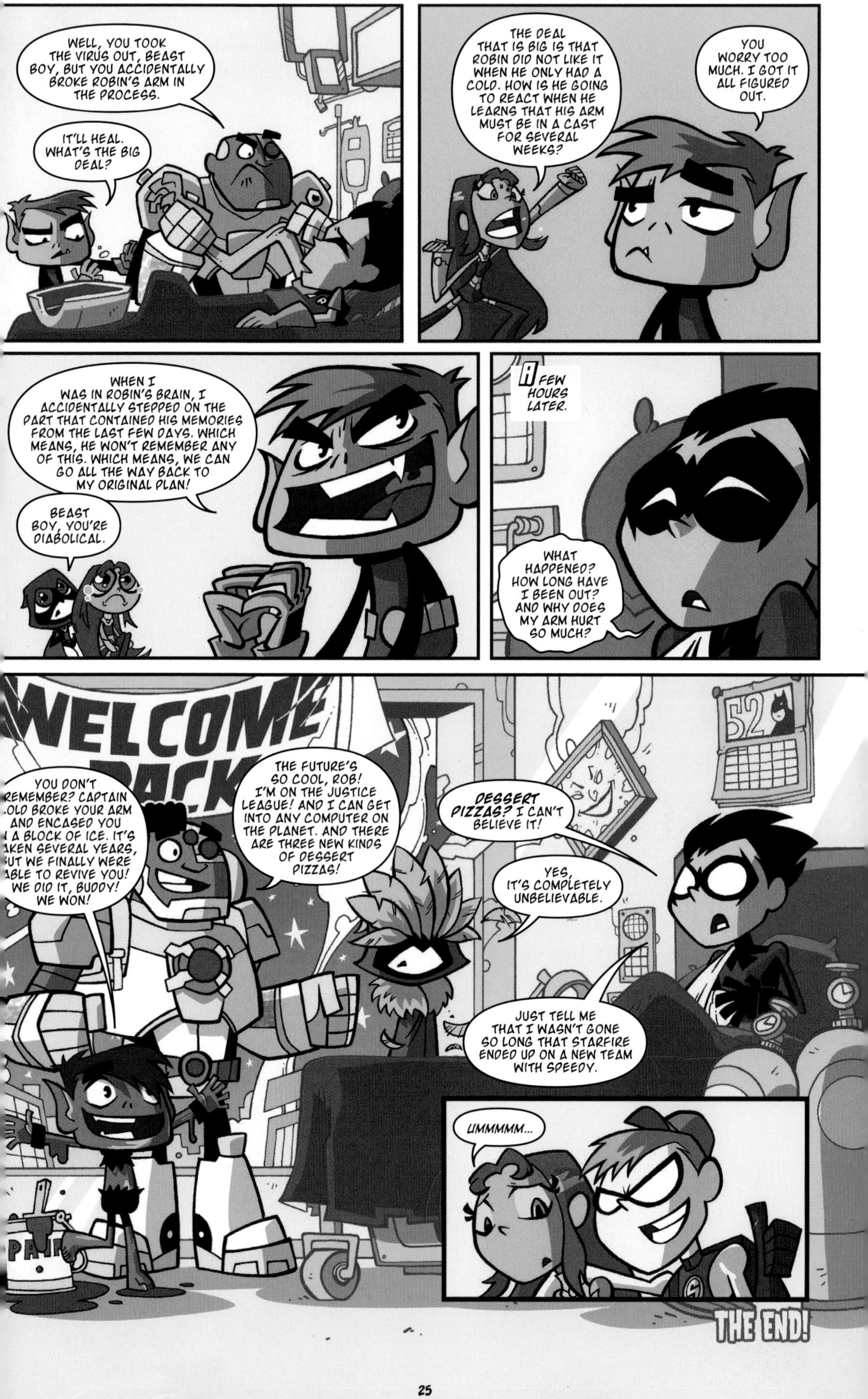
WELL, YOU TOOK THE VIRUS OUT, BEAST BOY, BUT YOU ACCIDENTALLY BROKE ROBIN'S ARM IN THE PROCESS.
IT'LL HEAL. WHAT'S THE BIG DEAL?
THE DEAL THAT IS BIG IS THAT ROBIN DID NOT LIKE IT WHEN HE ONLY HAD A COLD. HOW IS HE GOING TO REACT WHEN HE LEARNS THAT HIS ARM MUST BE IN A CAST FOR SEVERAL WEEKS?
YOU WORRY TOO MUCH. I GOT IT ALL FIGURED OUT.
WHEN I WAS IN ROBIN'S BRAIN, I ACCIDENTALLY STEPPED ON THE PART THAT CONTAINED HIS MEMORIES FROM THE LAST FEW DAYS. WHICH MEANS, HE WON'T REMEMBER ANY OF THIS. WHICH MEANS, WE CAN GO ALL THE WAY BACK TO MY ORIGINAL PLAN!
BEAST BOY, YOU'RE DIABOLICAL.
A FEW HOURS LATER.
WHAT HAPPENED? HOW LONG HAVE I BEEN OUT? AND WHY DOES MY ARM HURT SO MUCH?
WELCOME
YOU DON'T REMEMBER? CAPTAIN OLD BROKE YOUR ARM AND ENCASED YOU A BLOCK OF ICE. IT'S AKEN SEVERAL YEARS, UT WE FINALLY WERE ABLE TO REVIVE YOU! WE DID IT, BUDDY! WE WON!
THE FUTURE'S SO COOL, ROB! I'M ON THE JUSTICE LEAGUE! AND I CAN GET INTO ANY COMPUTER ON THE PLANET. AND THERE ARE THREE NEW KINDS OF DESSERT PIZZAS!
DESSERT PIZZAS? I CAN'T BELIEVE IT!
YES, IT'S COMPLETELY UNBELIEVABLE.
52
JUST TELL ME THAT I WASN'T GONE SO LONG THAT STARFIRE ENDED UP ON A NEW TEAM WITH SPEEDY.
UMMMMM...
THE END!

CREATORS

SHOLLY FISCH

Bitten by a radioactive typewriter, Sholly Fisch has spent the wee hours writing books, comics, TV scripts, and online material for over 25 years. His comic book credits include more than 200 stories and features about characters such as Batman, Superman, Bugs Bunny, Daffy Duck, Spider-Man, and Ben 10. Currently, he writes stories for Action Comics every month, plus stories for Looney Tunes and Scooby-Doo. By day, Sholly is a mild-mannered developmental psychologist who helps to create educational TV shows, web sites, and other media for kids.

MERRILL HAGAN

Merrill Hagan is a writer who as worked on numerous episodes of the hit *Teen Titans Go!* TV show. In addition, he has authored several *Teen Titans Go!* comic books and was a writer for the original *Teen Titans* series in 2003.

LEA HERNANDEZ

Lea Hernandez is a comic book artist and webcomic creator who is known for her manga-influenced style. She has worked with Marvel Comics, Oni Press, NBM Publishing, and DC Comics. In addition to her work on *Teen Titans Go!*, she is the co-creator of *Killer Princesses* and the creator of *Rumble Girls*.

JORGE CORONA

Jorge Corona is a Venezuelan comic artist who is well-known for his all-ages fantasy-adventure series *Feathers* and his work on *Jim Henson's The Storyteller: Dragons*. In addition to *Teen Titans Go!*, he has also worked on *Batman Beyond*, *Justice League Beyond*, *We Are Robin*, *Goners*, and many other comics.

GLOSSARY

a cappella (ah-kah-PELL-uh)—relating to singing without instrumentation

associate (uh-SOH-she-eht)—a partner or coworker

broadcast (BRAHD-kast)—a television or radio program

calisthenics (cal-is-THEN-iks)—exercises for getting fit

condemn (kuhn-DEM)—to force someone to suffer something unpleasant

derive (di-RIVE)—to take or receive something

diabolical (dye-uh-BOL-ik-uhl)—extremely wicked

eternal (i-TUR-nuhl)—a seemingly endless time period

GPS (GEE-PEE-ESS)—an electronic tool used to find the location of an object

humiliation (hyoo-mil-ee-AYE-shuhn)—a feeling of embarrassment or foolishness

implant (im-PLANT)—to put a device into the body by surgery

interpretive dance (in-TUR-pruh-tive DANSS)—a type of dance that shows emotions or tells a story

jinx (JINGKS)—to bring bad luck

microbe (MYE-krobe)—a living thing that is too small to see without a microscope

mime (MIME)—a performer who expresses himself or herself without words

mucous (MYOO-kuhss)—a slimy, thick fluid

paparazzi (pah-puh-RAHT-see)—aggressive photographers who take pictures of celebrities for sale to magazines or newspapers

pun (PUHN)—a play on words involving the deliberate confusion of similar words or phrases

ridicule (RID-uh-kyool)—harsh criticism or teasing

sanity (SAN-eh-tee)—the ability to think and behave in a normal manner

self-esteem (SELF-ess-TEEM)—a feeling of pride and respect for oneself

simian (SIM-ee-uhn)—relating to monkeys or apes

surpass (sur-PASS)—to be greater or stronger than another person or thing

torment (TOR-ment)—great pain and suffering

virus (VYE-ruhss)—a germ that infects living things and causes diseases

whimsy (WIM-zee)—playful or fanciful behavior

witness (WIT-niss)—to see something happen

VISUAL QUESTIONS & WRITING PROMPTS

1. Why does Robin change his mind about performing on the reality TV show? What clues in these panels support your answer?

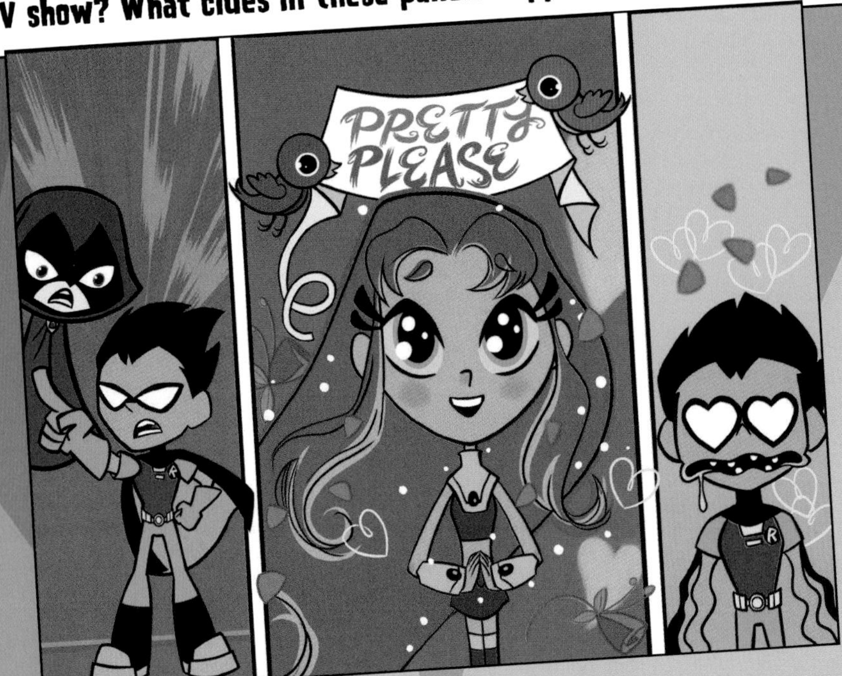
PRETTY PLEASE

2. Why are the Teen Titans drawn differently in this panel? How does the art style reflect how they are feeling?

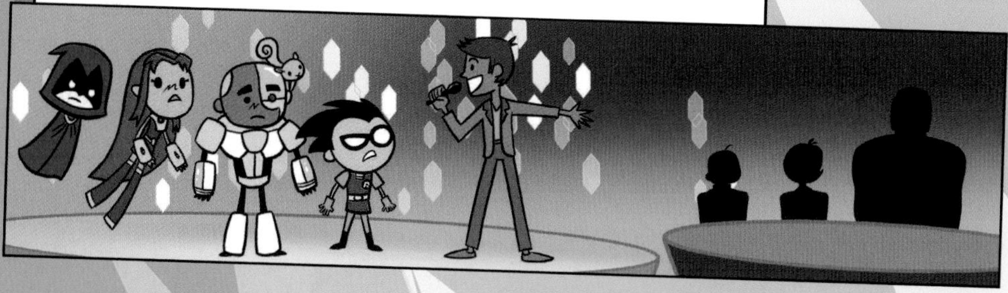

3. Make a list of things Robin keeps in his room. What kinds of interests and hobbies does he have? Discuss how you know.

4. Based on the shape of Robin's arm, what do you think Beast Boy turned into? Explain why you think so.

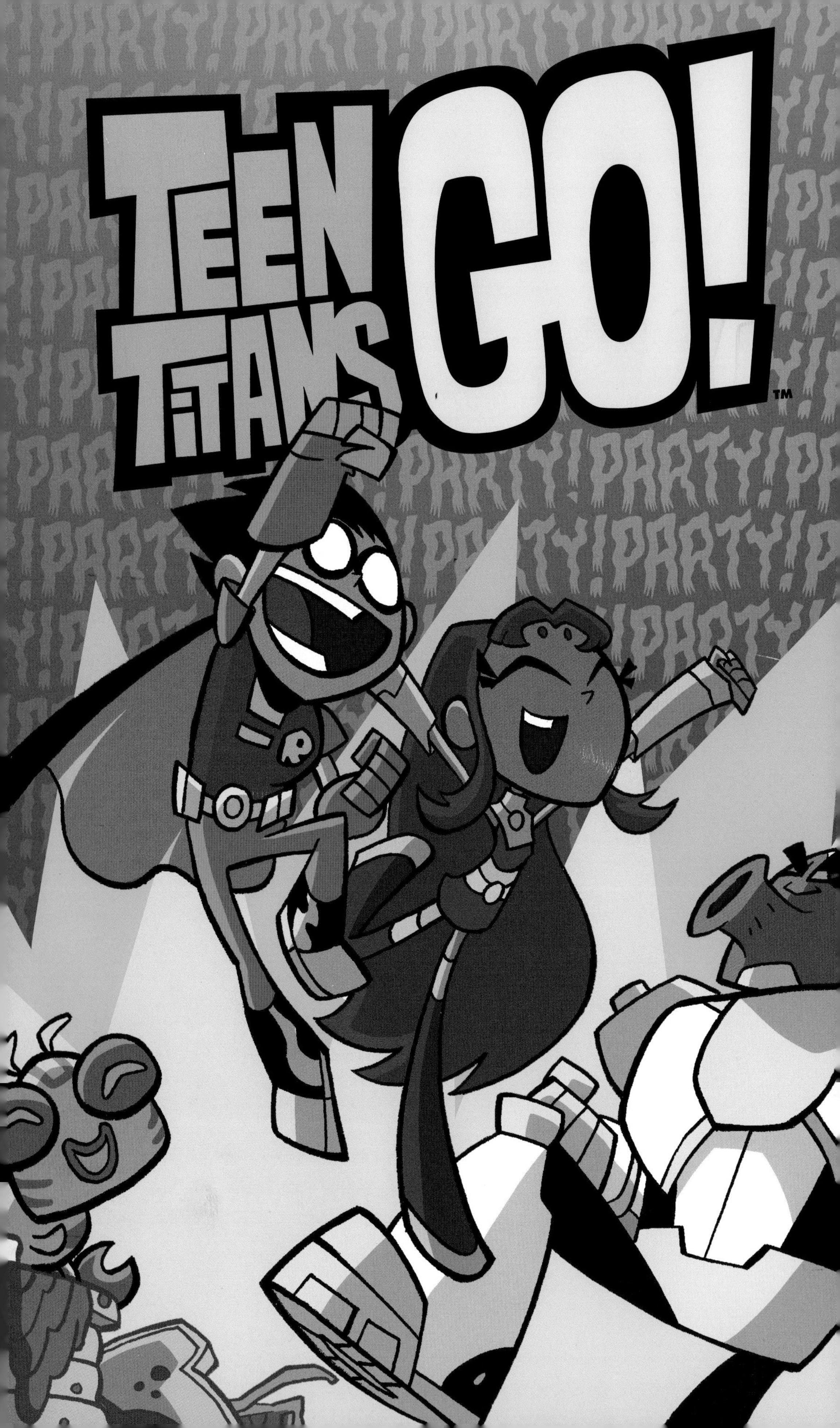
TEEN TITANS GO!™
PARTY! PARTY!

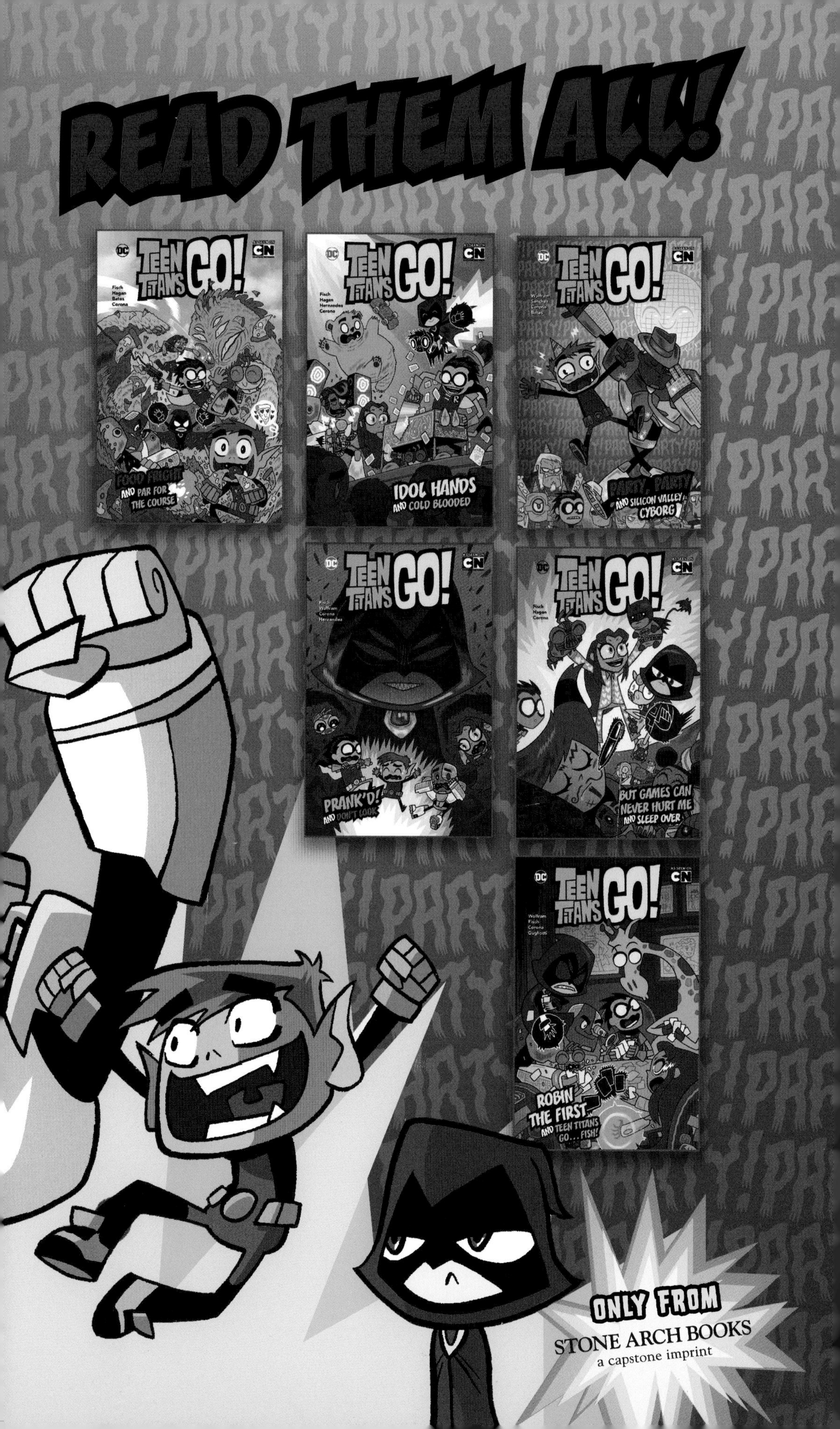
READ THEM ALL!
TEEN TITANS GO!
FOOD FRIGHT AND PAR FOR THE COURSE
TEEN TITANS GO!
IDOL HANDS AND COLD BLOODED
TEEN TITANS GO!
PARTY, PARTY AND SILICON VALLEY CYBORG
TEEN TITANS GO!
PRANK'D! AND DON'T LOOK
TEEN TITANS GO!
BUT GAMES CAN NEVER HURT ME AND SLEEP OVER
TEEN TITANS GO!
ROBIN THE FIRST AND TEEN TITANS GO... FISH!
ONLY FROM
STONE ARCH BOOKS
a capstone imprint

TEEN TITANS GO!™

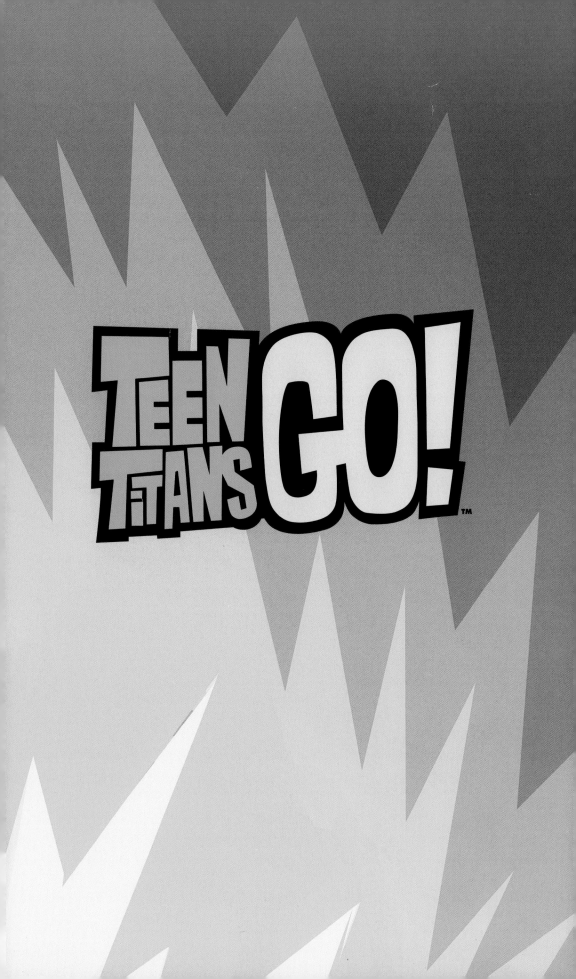